SO DEADLY MY LOVE

STEPHEN RANSOME

THE MYSTERY BOOK GUILD
178-202 GREAT PORTLAND STREET
LONDON, W.1

First published by
Victor Gollancz, 1957

This edition 1959

This book has been printed in Great Britain
by litho-offset on Antique Wove paper by
Taylor Garnett Evans & Co. Ltd., Watford,
Hertfordshire, and bound by them

CHAPTER I

Since sunset, especially since the moonless darkness had closed in, the Armstead home on Belle Loma
Drive had been a place of waiting stretched thin.

With the slow passing of the hours the three men in the
living-room had spoken to one another less and less, almost
as if fearing that the vibrations of their voices might disturb a delicate balance of forces and bring a catastrophe
crashing down. It was past midnight now, and still. Stillness and dread were the essence of this endless night, the
third since Lynn's disappearance.

The oldest of the three, the solidly built man standing
with his back to the curtained picture window, was Lynn's
father, Spencer Armstead. He had a look of strength, but
his unrelieved anxiety had brought a tremor to his hands
and a heartsick pallor to his face. He had managed to
sleep through a few of the past sixty-odd hours, refusing a
sedative, insisting he must remain on instant call. His eyes,
black brown behind black shell-rimmed glasses, gazing
through a mist of exhaustion, were blinking at the telephone—first at the phone, then at the portable tape recorder sitting alongside it.

The recorder was turned on, ready to spin into action,
with the selector switch set at *Stop*. The indicator light had
been glowing steadily, a wide-open green eye, around the
clock and around again since early Monday afternoon, an
eternity ago.

So far the recorder had been of no use whatever. Spencer Armstead hoped it might prove useful and despaired
that it would be of any good at all. Like the plans they had

thought out so carefully, it could do nothing more than wait in a vacuum for the message that might come at last in some other way.

The two other men, seated at a small square table, were frowning over the chess pieces of carved ivory on the inlaid board between them. Tense and tired, they had scarcely stirred in minutes. Now the taller and thinner straightened his stooped shoulders, pulling his thoughts back from a distance, and lifted his lean face for an inquisitive look at his opponent.

"Your move, isn't it?" Richard Carrick said softly.

Carrick, formerly a special agent for the FBI, was Spencer Armstead's attorney. He had a busy law office in Palmport, the city across the bay, and a smaller one here in Belle Loma. His manner usually was one of quiet and pleasant self-confidence, but tonight, faced with uncontrollable uncertainties, his natural cheerfulness was clouded over.

The other man hadn't heard.

"Tim, my friend, it's your move."

"Um? I did move, Dick. Didn't I?"

"No. Your move."

"Sorry. Can't seem to keep my mind off other things."

Timothy Hampden forced himself to reconsider a confused predicament among his chessmen. He was an estate agent whose name was becoming well known hereabouts; it was posted on a scattering of houses and apartment buildings in this Gulf Beach section of Florida. *Buy— Hampden Exclusive. Rent—Hampden Exclusive.* Tonight he was here not only as a friend and neighbour, but chiefly because he could not decently have been shut out of Spencer Armstead's confidence. The local police could be held off, and the newspapers kept in ignorance, and had been, but not Tim Hampden. Early last Monday morning, under circumstances which were still not clear, Tim's younger

6

brother Hal had been found brutally injured and unconscious, lying in a drenching rain in the street beside Lynn's empty car.

Hampden advanced his king's bishop almost aimlessly, and this small action triggered another on the part of Spencer Armstead. Lynn's father walked away from the phone, turned, walked, and stopped at the table. Although he was an ardent chess player, he had taken no interest in the game in progress; he ignored it now.

"The all-important thing is to get my little girl back home," he stated wretchedly. "Above everything else, get her back safely, safely."

Carrick and Hampden looked up at him, their sympathy tempered with a trace of annoyance. How many times since calling on them for advice and help—— How many times had they heard him reiterate those same words? He had emphasized the point endlessly, over and over. Of course they agreed—it was desperately important to see Lynn returned unharmed, and they were trying their best to ensure just that. But Spencer Armstead's "little girl" was twenty-six years old. She was a married woman —technically married, at any rate, separated from her husband. Despite all Spence's pampering, and even though she was an only child, Lynn Armstead Griffith was an unspoiled, self-reliant young adult.

"I've done everything they asked. I've followed their instructions to the letter. They must have known damned well I wouldn't try any tricks, not with Lynn's life at stake. I've kept faith, I've done every single damned thing they asked. They've had the money twenty hours now. Why haven't they sent a message? What more do they want me to do?"

Carrick said patiently, as patiently as he had said it several times before, "There's nothing more anyone can do, Spence, except go on waiting."

"It's still too early," Tim Hampden reminded him matter-of-factly. "It'll be hours."

Spencer Armstead made an angry sound, and as he swung back to glare at the telephone again Tim Hampden frowned after him. Carrick saw the hurt in Hampden's eyes and read the thought behind it. Hal Hampden was lying in Palmport Hospital with a fractured skull and serious internal injuries, with pneumonia a complication. It was touch and go with Hal; he had only a slim chance of pulling through. Somehow the same violence that had snatched Lynn away had left Hal very nearly killed. At times Spence seemed to have forgotten that, but it was only because he was too distracted by his anxiety for his daughter to feel much concern for anyone else.

Hampden shrugged as if thinking, *You have to take Spence as he comes; it's no use blaming him for being what he is,* and turned back to the uninteresting, time-killing game.

Looking at Hampden, Carrick shook his head gently. It was being hellish tough on both of them. Tim was numb with worry about his brother, naturally, but at least he was being kept fully informed as to Hal's condition. Spence, on the other hand, was utterly in the dark about what might have happened to Lynn since the early morning of last Monday. Tim did not know whether his brother would live or die; Spence had absolutely no way of knowing whether or not his daughter was already dead. As matters stood, neither of them had or could have the slightest control over the conclusion. Neither could know which way the scales would tip until time told them—for Tim, Carrick thought, a longer time than for Spence. Spence would probably be the first to learn the answer. If a definite break was in store for him, it would come tonight.

"God, if we only had her back home!" Spencer Armstead blurted in a surge of rage. "If only we could get started after the dirty savages who did this to her!" Remembering, he turned to Tim Hampden. "And to Hal. I'll get them for this damnable outrage. If it takes the rest of my life, I'll *get them!*"—fist smacking into palm.

He had said this before, too, a dozen times or more in the past three days, in almost the same words. They knew he didn't mean to sound melodramatic. This was a sincere expression of his embracing apprehension for Lynn and an effort to relieve some of the unbearable stresses within himself. Nothing since her mother's death had been too good for Lynn—conversely, no punishment could be too severe upon those who had dared to harm her. They had no doubt that he meant wholeheartedly every bitter word.

For the third time in as many minutes Spencer Armstead peered at his wrist-watch, making sure it was still ticking. He stood near the telephone, his eyes smarting with his long-denied need for sleep. Small sounds accentuated the quiet. He listened to them. Remembering that the first note had been slipped under the front door and the second found in the grass near the rear patio, he tried hopefully to read meaning into them.

The hum of a car passing and turning at the corner towards Gulf Boulevard. . . . Out on the bay the sudden *chrr-r* of a motor-boat getting under way. The boat put on speed and the noises faded off towards the north, where there were many private piers along the bay front. . . . The breeze surging off the Gulf of Mexico was disturbing the cabbage palms along the Drive; the continuous rattling of the fronds would mask the sounds of any stealthy approach. . . . Spencer Armstead would not permit himself to think that the third and final message, telling him where to find Lynn, might not come at all. It must come. But how? And when? God above, *when?*

At the chess table Tim Hampden said wearily, "Your move, Dick."

"What?"

"Your move this time."

"That's right, so it is."

Just as Carrick closed his finger-tips on a pawn the telephone shrilled.

Spencer Armstead's hand sprang to a grip on the instrument. Instantly Carrick was out of his chair. Lynn's father compelled himself to wait the few seconds it took Carrick to reach the tape recorder and click the switch over to *Record*. The two plastic reels were turning now, the brown ribbon flowing past the recording head. Spencer Armstead lifted the receiver, drawing an unsteady breath.

A look of sharper affliction took hold of his face. His disappointment brought nausea. He said brokenly, "Yes —yes, he's—here," and pushed the phone into Carrick's hands.

Carrick knew it was Julia, and why. He hadn't finished saying hello before she began, her voice raised on a familiar note of complaint.

"Dick, you promised you'd be home early. Early, you said, you promised faithfully, and here it is a whole half-hour past midnight."

Carrick turned the switch back, and the reels of the recorder stopped. Sometimes he wished there were such a switch on Julia herself; it would be a blessing. He knew what their friends thought, what Tim and Spence were probably thinking now. *Julia was such a lovely and sweet girl when Dick married her and she's turned into such a bitch. Feel sorry for the poor guy.* He knew that and resented it. Julia at her best was still as lovely and sweet as any woman could be. It was just that she was too careless about letting others see her at her worst.

"Dick, why don't you answer me?"

The sudden loud ring of the bell had drained his breath for a moment. "I'm here, Julie."

"That's just the whole trouble. You're there when you

should be at home where you belong. You *know* I'm frightened to be left all alone in this house at night. Promising you won't be late, then staying out till all hours! I do think you might be a little more considerate."

"I didn't realize," Carrick said, "but I'm about through now."

"I should hope so. I can't see why you don't get your work finished during office hours. Is this—this—whatever you're doing for Spence—is it so much more important than being at home with your wife?"

It was, yes. He said nothing, which was his way of letting her know she had said too much. Now she would turn contrite; she always did. It wasn't an act either; she sincerely regretted these outbursts of self-pity. The trouble was, the regret didn't last long enough to forestall the next one.

"Dick, darling, I'm terribly sorry; I'm being awful, a perfect shrew. But honestly, I've been so lonely for you, and worried, too, thinking something might have happened to you on the way. You won't be very much longer, will you, darling? I'm so edgy I couldn't think of going to bed without you."

Spencer Armstrong was scowling, his eyes turned from Carrick; but his dark look was a demand. *Get her off the line. Keep that line open!*

"Leaving now, Julie. Be there in a few minutes."

She gave a long sigh. "You don't know how happy I'll be to have you close to me, sweetheart."

He hung up, realizing he hadn't been entirely fair to Julie about this. She had asked him why he was spending so much time with Spence this week, and he hadn't told her the truth. Spence had insisted she wasn't to know Lynn was missing—certainly a reasonable precaution; Julie couldn't keep a secret. He had given her a vague excuse about contracts being drawn up, a complicated and confidential deal, something he couldn't let her in on just yet. She had been the forbearing wife for two nights; but three nights in a row——

"No help for it, I've got to go. I'll stay with her until she's asleep, then come back." Julie wouldn't know he had gone out again. She would slumber like the dead and wake up saying she hadn't slept a wink. "As Tim said, Spence, we have several more hours to go, probably."

"They're playing it safe, too, naturally," Hampden said. "Still too many people up and around."

Carrick nodded thoughtfully. "They might be watching this place. That's easy to do, from both the bay and the Drive. They may have seen us coming in. If so, they may not move as long as Tim and I are here."

"I think Dick's right," Hampden said. "This is risky as hell for them, you know. They're handling dynamite and don't dare slip. They may suspect a trap. If both of us clear out you may hear from them sooner."

"As far as our going into action is concerned, Spence, it won't matter very much—won't make more than a few minutes' difference. Anyhow I have to go if Julie's to be kept quiet. As soon as you hear, call me"—the bell wouldn't waken Julie, it never did—"and I'll get here faster than a bat."

"I could use a little sleep," Hampden said. "I'll catch a nap in my clothes. Less than a block away—I can make it in two minutes by the clock. Meanwhile you'll be all right here, Spence."

"Here's another thought." Carrick gestured towards the tape recorder. "They can't know for certain your line is tapped, but they may be afraid of the possibility. If they're going to use the phone tonight, they might be waiting to relay the message through Tim or me."

"Yes," Spencer Armstead said heavily. "I can depend on both of you, I'm sure of that. You've both shown yourselves to be the best of friends. Yes, I'll be all right alone here. It won't do any harm and it may help. Anything, anything that might help——"

They were moving towards the vestibule. Abruptly they stopped, looking quickly at one another, caught by surprise.

A gong had sounded. The front door.

CHAPTER II

JOHN GRIFFITH HAD left his truck in the parking lot of the Beachcomber Bar on Gulf Boulevard. The Armstead home being only two short blocks away, he had walked. The few beers he had gulped hadn't calmed him at all, and he had thought the walk might help him to get a better grip on himself. Merely thinking about Lynn had made him shaky—realizing that every step was bringing him closer to a big decision, one that would be a crucial turning-point in both their lives.

He had started off on impulse, but on reaching the wrought-iron gate in the brick fence he had dragged to a stop. He had felt highly hopeful that Lynn would agree to another try, yet he had been panicky, too, knowing her way of sticking with her convictions. He had stayed there on the sidewalk several minutes, thinking over what he would say to her. Moving back and forth, softly whistling a fragment of a tune—an unconscious habit in moments of caution—he had felt an inward trembling of anticipation mixed with a kind of stage fright.

Why, he had wondered, why did he have to be the highly-strung type, so easily keyed up? Anybody looking at him would take him to be just the opposite, steady and easy-going. Watching him on the job, seeing his boxer's shoulders, his washboard belly, and his sunbrown that couldn't get any browner, they'd say Griff hadn't a nerve in his body. All the hard physical work he did for a living, sinking piling, building sea walls and groins, knocking piers together—a rock of a guy. Well, he wasn't that kind at all, not inside. At such a time as this, a time of self-commitment—like the day he'd married Lynn, and before that, when he'd plunged his last nickel into buying the option on Pelican Key—he turned jumpy as a cat.

While getting hold of himself he had watched the Armstead home. Lynn's upstairs bedroom was dark and its windows were closed. The lamps in the living-room below were shining dimly through the drawn curtains. The whole house had seemed—aloof. It was like Lynn's father, impressively big and rich, a solid shelter, comforting to those who belonged, formidable to outsiders. It had given Griff a sense that, for him personally and specially, it was out of bounds.

Rebelling against that feeling, he had opened the gate quickly. Half-way down the long gravel walk he had hesitated again for half a second. Two cars were sitting alongside the house, visible in the glow from a nearby window, and Griff hadn't, offhand, recognized one of them. Probably a visitor's. No matter; he wasn't stopping now, not for anybody. He had come straight on to the door and had given the bell-button a stiff-fingered poke.

That hard knot of a thing in his throat, he told himself ruefully while waiting, was his pride. He'd had a tough time getting it swallowed, but at least it was half-way down. It hurt, but now that he was here, the bell rung, the die cast, it would have to go down the rest of the way and stay there for keeps.

The entrance light flashed on, and as the door opened Griff saw Spencer Armstead doing a peculiar thing. Instead of looking straight out, as he normally would, Lynn's father looked down at the sill as if expecting to find something there. He even stooped a little, in a hurry to pick it up. Not finding it, whatever it might have been, he straightened with an expression of despair on his face; and when he saw Griff he stood there scowling in his confusion.

"I know it's late," Griff said. "Strange time to come calling, but—— Mind if I come in for a minute?"

Spencer Armstead's answer was slow in coming. His attitude made it clear that Griff was not welcome. Spencer Armstead said, "I was just going to bed."

"I hadn't expected you to be up this late. I thought Lynn—— Anyhow——"

"What do you want?"

This show of impatience and opposition was just what Griff needed. It was something he could organize himself against. He began feeling steadier now, on solider ground.

"It's important. To Lynn and me both. Very important."

Spencer Armstead turned back resignedly and Griff went in. It was the first time he had seen this room in months. Not that he had missed coming here; he had never felt at home in Spencer Armstead's house. And never less than now. Pointedly, Lynn's father did not invite him to sit.

Griff glanced around. At the front door, just as he punched the bell-button, he had thought he heard voices. There was no one here, though—he and Lynn's father were alone in the room.

"Lynn?" Spencer Armstead asked. "What about Lynn?"

"I've got to see her." Griff said it urgently. "Talk to her. That's all."

"It can wait."

"No, sir."

"It will have to wait. You can't see her."

"*Can't?*"

"Lynn is not here."

"But her car's here," Griff said reasonably. "Coming in, I saw it. It's right out there in the carport now."

Spencer Armstead had no answer for that. Either he was at a loss for one—for a moment he had seemed to be— or else he was bluntly refusing all co-operation.

Lynn's father had opposed her marriage to Griff; he had never resigned himself to it, and Griff knew he was thoroughly satisfied to see them separated. Griff had expected no friendliness from him, much less encouragement. That was all right; Lynn had a mind of her own, and Griff was seeking a reconciliation with her, not Spencer Armstead. He hadn't expected, though, to run into anything quite as thick as this.

"Sir, I know you don't like me. You don't want me anywhere near Lynn. I understand that. But you can't keep us from seeing each other if——"

"Lynn is not here," Spencer Armstead said again flatly. "That settles the matter, doesn't it? For now, at least?"

"Where is she?"

It was a simple, natural question. Why should it bring such a flash of fury to Spencer Armstead's eyes?

"She's—out of town," Lynn's father said, looking away. "Visiting friends."

"Which friends?"

"The—Courtenays."

The Courtenays lived near Bonita Springs, about half a day's drive southward on Route 41, the Tamiami Trail. Lynn would have used her car. But her car was here. . . . Another thing. The Courtenays' place was an isolated one, back on the fringe of the Everglades, and they had no telephone. There wasn't any way Griff could reach Lynn there except by driving down himself. And since he was a

16

working man, putting in long hours, busy on a hurry-up
job——

"When will she be back?"

Another natural, logical question, yet to Lynn's father it
seemed as painful as a twisting knife. Griff saw the ridged
tendons in his jaw, his straining effort to hold himself under
control.

"I don't know," Spencer Armstead said, a hoarseness in
his voice. "Soon, I hope. In a few days—at the most. I'll
tell her you want to see her." He glared at Griff. "Good
night."

Griff didn't move. Something was wrong here. There
was something very wrong with Spencer Armstead and
this whole place tonight.

"Has anything happened to Lynn?"

"No, no!" Spencer Armstead said quickly. "No! Of
course not. I told you, she's simply out of town, visiting
friends. Griff, I'm not feeling well. Please go now."

"I'm sorry, sir. You do look worn out. Extremely worried about something. If it's Lynn—— Is she sick? Has
she had an accident? I've a right to know. She's still my
wife."

Griff was startled by the flush of rage to Spencer Armstead's face.

"There's nothing more to tell you! Nothing! Can't you
understand that?"

Spencer Armstead looked angry enough to throw him
bodily out of the house. Griff stood his ground, bewildered, looking around the room again. Something seemed
changed. There was something different about it tonight.
Griff's gaze settled on the wide accordion door stretching
between the fireplace and the front wall. The corner room
beyond was one for informal relaxation—Lynn called it
the family room—furnished with a small bar, a record
player, a TV console. If Griff had ever seen that accordion

door completely closed, he couldn't remember. But it was closed now, all the way. . . . Hiding something?

A game of chess had been interrupted. Lynn's father evidently had been playing with one of his friends earlier this evening. It wasn't like Spencer Armstead to abandon a game—his strategy was to play it through, no matter how late the hour might grow, in order to wear his opponent down. . . . And that tape recorder on the desk. Griff had seen it before; it belonged to Dick Carrick. It was turned on, ready for use. So far as Griff could recall, Lynn's father knew nothing about operating a tape recorder.

"You're in some kind of trouble," Griff said. "Aren't you? Either you or Lynn? If it's Lynn—— She's still my wife and I've got to know——"

"See here, Griff!" Spencer Armstead snapped it out. "Lynn left you more than three months ago. Your marriage is over, done. She's had the divorce papers drawn up and they're ready to serve. The rest is a simple legal routine. Stop calling her your wife. She's no longer any concern of yours."

"Yes, sir, she is. She certainly is. She'll always be." At the mention of the divorce papers Griff had felt his face turn prickly cold. "That's why I've got to get things settled between us."

"It's already settled. There's nothing more to be said about it. Griff, I've asked you to leave."

Griff gazed at him steadily. "I'm not leaving without an answer. Is Lynn in any kind of trouble? Is she all right?"

"Lynn is not in any kind of trouble." Spencer Armstead wrung the words out of himself. "She's perfectly all right."

"Okay. But I'm still going to see her as soon as possible. I'll be back when——"

18

A clattering noise startled Griff. He looked quickly at the closed accordion door. The sound had come from inside the family room. Lynn? Could it be possible Lynn was in there, hiding, avoiding him while her father stood him off?

Impulse propelled Griff before he had given himself time to think. When his hands were on the door, sliding it open, the realization caught up with him that it wouldn't be at all like Lynn to do such a childish thing—she would always have the courage to face him. By that time he was already looking into the room.

It was dark except for the light fanning in. He saw two men in chairs. Dick Carrick and Tim Hampden. The two of them sitting there in the dark! Carrick was stooping forward, frozen in the act of picking up an ash-tray that had fallen off the table at his elbow.

As Griff turned back to Lynn's father, Carrick and Hampden came quickly into the living-room.

"Let's have it straight now," Griff said. "No more double talk. What's wrong here?"

It was Carrick who answered him.

"There's no reason for you to be upset, Griff. This is all very simple. Tim and I were watching television. I switched off the set just as you came in. We stayed in there because this was a family matter. We couldn't help over-hearing, though—and I'm glad of it. For some reason you don't seem to trust what Spence told you about Lynn. I happen to be in a position to confirm it."

"That I'd like to hear!"

"The other day—last Monday morning it was—I had to drive down to Naples to see a client. Lynn wanted to get away, so she went with me as far as the Courtenays'. I expected to pick her up on my return trip, but as it happens the Courtenays will be driving up to Tarpon Springs in a few days. She'll come back with them—they'll drop her off here. That's all there is to it." Carrick smiled. "So there's absolutely nothing to worry about, Griff."

"Guess not," Griff said.

"Confidentially," Carrick added, "we *are* having a little trouble here, a bothersome piece of legal business, but it hasn't anything at all to do with Lynn."

"You're satisfied, I hope," Spencer Armstead said with heavy indignation. "I hope that settles it. Now get out of here."

"Okay, okay," Griff said.

He felt foolish. His face was hot. He turned on his heel.

Driving along Gulf Boulevard towards the business section of Belle Loma and his home beyond, Griff took with him a tangle of feelings. He was disheartened because he hadn't seen Lynn and angry with himself for wading in without having thought to phone first to make sure she was at home. He was abysmally let down. Half an hour ago he had been brimming with elation at the prospect of making a happy new start with Lynn; now all his hopes were left dangling in empty space. "Back in a few days" was too damn indefinite. A few days would seem twice as long as forever.

Griff didn't exactly resent Spencer Armstead's rancour —he had resigned himself to that long ago. Lynn's father, being as possessive and protective of her as he was, probably would have been jealous of any man she might have married, no matter who. But he had gone to an extreme tonight. The man was badly upset, obviously, and Griff, coming in at an unlucky moment, had caught the brunt by transference. That probably accounted for it, but Griff still couldn't understand why Spencer Armstead should get so overwrought over a "bothersome piece of legal business", or over any other sort of trouble if it had nothing to do with Lynn.

Dick Carrick had been reassuring enough, but—hadn't

he glossed it over a bit too smoothly? Gaining a perspective on it now, Griff saw that Carrick had explained hardly anything—Lynn's car, yes, but nothing else. Griff wasn't entitled to a fuller explanation, of course, so long as their "little trouble" did not include Lynn. But if she *was* involved, if they were covering up something about her, something serious—— The thought brought heat to Griff's face. If Lynn was really in trouble and they were deliberately keeping him in ignorance, lying to him——!

He squirmed under the possibility. Should he turn back and try again? . . . No; Carrick was as clever on his feet as Spencer Armstead was immovable. No, it would do no good. Griff couldn't get an answer from Lynn, either, until she returned with the Courtenays. But in the meantime he couldn't let it ride. He could damned well try to find out in some other way—do a little checking on his own.

Nearing the centre of Belle Loma, he noticed for the first time how dark the night was, and the intensity of the darkness deepened his uneasiness. The sky, usually a vast starspeckled luminescence, was blanketed by a thick overcast. On Griff's left the bay was all blackness except for the distant red flashing of the channel-marker off the northern tip of Pelican Key. The only lighted windows in sight were those on the corner of Eighteenth Street, just ahead, in the trim stucco building which housed the town offices, the volunteer fire-department and the police station all in one.

Dan Teague, the chief of police, might know something helpful, but Dan was rarely on duty at night—never, in fact, except in emergencies, which were few and far between. At this hour, quiet as it was, Dan would be at home and solidly in the sack. Griff decided to go in anyway. He'd see which one of the town's eight cops was holding down the graveyard watch and try a few questions.

Just inside the screen door Griff stopped short. Dan Teague was at his desk.

"Hello!" Griff said. "Hello, what's this?"

The chief of police of Belle Loma, brush-haired and husky, had been staring with a whole-minded intensity at nothing. In his sun-tan sport shirt, his snug matching trousers and shining black shoes, he looked neat, efficient and younger than his forty years. Always, even in the stickiest stretches of the long summer, Dan Teague managed to keep himself in military press. Always before, whenever Griff had dropped in, he had given out with the grinning, sincerely glad kind of greeting which good friends spontaneously have for each other. But not tonight. Griff was surprised all over again to find Teague aiming at him a look that said plainly as words, "What the hell are *you* doing here?"

"So?" Griff asked again. "What goes?"

Equally unusual was the fact that Teague took his time about responding, just as Spencer Armstead had done, and even then it was hardly an answer.

"A policeman's lot is not a happy one," he said, still gazing at Griff curiously. "Or hadn't you heard?"

"I can see that. Something's keeping you up long past your beddy-bye time. Something big must be cooking."

Teague wagged his head. "Like others among our good townspeople, you think a police chief has nothing to do but drain nickels out of the parking meters? Not so. There's paper work to do, among forty other things, a pile of it. I've been catching up with my paper work."

Teague's desk was clear—nothing there except the clean blotter and his spotless visored cap with his chief's badge pinned on it, precisely centred. No papers at all.

"Now that you've finished, why don't you go home?"

"In a minute. Duty comes first. For instance, a tax-paying citizen has just entered my office at an unusual hour. If you have a cup of coffee in mind, we're fresh out. If it's official, what can I do for you, sir?"

Griff was looking through a closed, glass-paned connecting door. There were four patrolmen in the next room, sleepily playing cards. Five men on call at this time of the night, including the chief himself! It was unheard of. Something especially important was on the fire all right, but whatever it was, Dan Teague had made it clear he intended to tell Griff nothing about it.

"I was on my way home and I'd got to thinking about Hal Hampden," Griff said, "—wondering how he is and what really happened to him."

It interested Dan Teague. He tilted his swivel chair far back, studying Griff's face soberly.

"Hal isn't particularly a pal of yours, is he, Griff?"

"Why, no. I don't run with his crowd. I'm more the unfancy type who pals around with Coast Guardsmen and cops. I just thought I'd ask. Anything new about him?"

"I guess you know Hal has dated Lynn more than once since you two split up."

In this little town news got around fast once it was started. Yes, Griff had heard that Lynn was going out with Hal frequently. He didn't like it, but he was in no position to object. It had been open and above-board, mostly dinners at the yacht club. Anyhow Lynn was well able to take care of herself, and Griff trusted her.

"She wasn't with Hal when it happened, was she?"

"What I know about it, Griff, isn't much more than everybody else knows. There's very little to add to what the papers have printed. There's talk going around town, naturally, there always is, but it's guesswork, irresponsible chatter. Hal's out cold, and has been all along, so we've had nothing from him directly. And if there were any witnesses, they haven't come forward." While saying all that,

Teague had seemed to be giving himself time to think just how to treat Griff's question. He was a smart officer, this Teague, well qualified for his job through training and experience. After hesitating a moment, he answered, "No, Lynn didn't have a date with Hal that night."

"You checked on it? With Lynn herself? When did you see her?"

"Didn't need to check with Lynn herself. Hal had been at a party at Majorca Beach, at the Mintons'. Not a big party, only six guests, and Lynn wasn't one of them. It started with supper and ran very late—very early, rather, into the early morning. Hal came alone and left alone. It happened on his way home. I hope he'll be able to tell us before long why he was waylaid and given such a damned vicious beating."

Dan Teague rose, moved around to the front of his desk, and sat on a corner of it.

"One of the few things we're sure of is that he wasn't robbed. That's the angle people are gossiping about the most. Whatever the motive was, it wasn't robbery."

"What was it, then?"

Teague looked at Griff for a moment, then answered with a brief shake of his head. Either he didn't know, or if he did he simply wasn't saying.

According to the first news account, Hal Hampden had been found by a man named Denty who was driving his regular newspaper route, angling his sedan in and out of streets, delivering *Tribunes*. It was raining so hard at the time that Denty had almost missed seeing Hal lying there in the gutter, partly under his sports coupé. Denty had called the Belle Loma police office from a nearby outdoor phone booth and had waited there until the ambulance arrived.

"About 5.30 a.m.," Griff remembered. "In the street alongside the bank building."

He was leading into an important question having to do with Lynn. She was a member of the Belle Loma Post of the Ground Observer Corps. Her regular once-a-week watch was on Sunday night, from midnight until four in the morning. She handled it alone because air traffic was light during that period, and in all their fifteen months of marriage she hadn't missed once. The post shelter was a hut on the roof of the bank building, directly above the spot where Hal Hampden had been struck down.

"Who was up there in the GOC post at the time?" Griff asked. "Didn't they notice anything?"

Again Teague shook his close-cropped head. "I checked on that first thing, trying to fix the time. Lynn went on duty at midnight and left a little before four, when her relief came up. Those plane spotters know how to listen, but there wasn't anything to notice—no unusual noise. Anyhow they keep their eyes on the sky, not on the street." The chief lowered his eyebrows at Griff. "Hal Hampden is no more than a casual acquaintance of yours. All these questions—it's Lynn you're really asking about. Any special reason?"

"I don't know," Griff said, feeling empty.

"Well, then, forget it."

Dan Teague took Griff's arm and steered him to the door. Griff suspected that Teague, expecting something to break soon, wanted to get rid of him before it did. He shrugged; as long as it had nothing to do with Lynn, he didn't care. But as the chief walked with him to his truck, he was dogged by unshakeable doubts. Teague hadn't lied to him outright, he didn't think that, but it was a damn sure thing the chief was holding something back for a peculiar reason. It might not be related to Lynn, or it might. But even if it was—just as in the case of Spencer Armstead and Dick Carrick—there was no way Griff could pull it out of him.

"Griff—— I mentioned there's talk going around. Don't pop your cork over this now, but some of it's about you. Hal was dating your wife, and even though Lynn and you are separated, some people seem to think you could have been sore enough about it to——"

"You're kidding!" Griff stared and saw that Teague wasn't kidding. "That's crazy!"

"Easy, boy. Nobody who knows you well would think you're *that* hot-headed. Take me, for example. I haven't questioned you about it, have I, or made you try to account for yourself? Well, remember that, if you happen to hear it from somebody else, and keep your head on."

"Sure. Thanks for telling me." Griff was stunned by the unthinking senselessness of it. Beating up a good friend of Lynn's would hardly help to persuade her to come back to living with him.

"Besides," Teague reminded him, "Lynn and Hal were not out on a date together at the time."

"Thanks, Dan," Griff said again, dazedly.

"Don't mention it." Teague whacked Griff's shoulder. "Ouch. Muscles like iron bands," and he chuckled. "Good night, Griff."

"'Night," Griff said absently.

He had learned nothing here. He was wondering where to turn next. Wasn't there anything else he could do besides wait—wait days for Lynn to come back with the Courtenays?

Chief of Police Dan Teague, watching Griff driving away, drew in a slow breath. It hadn't been easy, dodging Griff's anxious questions. Nor had it been easy these past three days to sit still and do nothing under the obdurate demands of a frantic and influential father. This case *must* be nearing the cracking-point now. He hoped it wouldn't be much longer before the expected call from Spencer

Armstead would release them all from this chafing in-action.

Turning back to continue his vigil, Teague saw the headlamps of a parked car light up in the next block, north of Nineteenth Street. He watched the car coming straight on, and as it passed under the street lamp on the corner he recognized the driver.

"*That's* funny," he said to himself. "Dick Carrick keeping an eye on Griff. Ex-FBI man tailing Lynn's husband."

CHAPTER III

For hour after hour she had been drifting on a rising and falling tide of pain, in and out of a cave of sleep.

For Lynn Griffith, these past three days and nights, sleep had been without restfulness, a sick kind of partial extinction. She was lying awkwardly on her back, as she had been lying interminably since they had brought her here. She could change her position only by drawing up her knees or by laboriously rolling herself over on her opposite shoulder. It would ease her distress a little, but not for long. Soon the bone-deep aching of her arms and legs and back would begin ascending again into a body-filling torment.

Wakening, she would struggle to free herself. The bonds at her ankles, and at her wrists crossed behind her, held her unbreakably, but each time she would try again until her strength was gone. Then the blankness would cloud back once more and close mercifully over her mind.

Each time she tried to hold the blankness with her; but suddenly now she threw it off. She lifted her head and held her breath, trying to reach past the limits of her awareness.

. . . He was coming back. She could see nothing at all and had heard no sound, but she knew. She *felt* him coming.

She knew it in the only way left to her. They had carefully blocked all her normally used paths of perception. A sticky strip of tape was stretched across her eyes, adhering from temple to temple, from eyebrows to cheekbones. Both her ears were closed by wads of some sort of pliable substance crammed into them. When there were sounds to hear she could barely discern them—now and then, dimly, the exhaust of a motor-boat passing at a distance she could not estimate. But short of keeping her heavily drugged, they could not rob her of all her sensitivities. She had learned to become increasingly conscious of subtle signals which ordinarily she would not have noticed.

She knew it was long past midnight now; her skin had told her. The heat of the daytime had ebbed away; a growing coolness in the air had meant the night was passing. Her dress was light cotton, she was without any kind of covering, and she was shivering—this was the night at its coolest. It must be an hour or two before dawn, their prowling time, and now he was coming back.

She lay with her whole body tight, feeling faint vibrations in the floor, a series of beats evenly spaced. A man walking. The silent beats grew slightly stronger as he came closer. . . . Now he had stopped; he was standing still outside this structure—whatever her prison was—probably looking all around, making certain he was not seen.

She rested her head on the floor, waiting, dreading to feel him moving again. This man was the hateful one, the one she loathed and feared.

From the first there had been two of them acting together, never at any time more than two, and she had learned to recognize each by his footfalls and by the way he used his hands. One of them moved quietly, and when he took hold of her he did it with a certain gentleness. She had come to believe he would not intentionally hurt her. If she was going to die, it would be the other who would kill her—the one standing outside now.

His was an arrogant way of walking, his pace direct, the impact of his heels cocksure. His hands gripped quickly and contemptuously. She thought of him as being secretly a coward, the kind who turned sadistic when his victim could not fight back. Since the first morning he had held a vindictive grudge against her. In a moment of terrified defiance she had exposed him to the danger of discovery, and he hadn't stopped punishing her for it with his bullying roughness.

He had come in alone, late that first morning, and she had sensed his haste and impatience. Grabbing her arms, he had lifted her shoulders and twisted her about so that she leaned against the wall. She had waited in breathless apprehension for minutes, not knowing what he meant to do next.

Then he had come back and fumbled with one end of the length of adhesive tape strapped across her mouth. His careless finger-nails had scratched her cheek, and suddenly he had yanked the strip off. The stinging pain had stiffened her. Next she had felt something pushing at her lips. Pressing them together against the prodding, she had smelled an odour of food and had realized he was trying to feed her. Still she had resisted, thinking wildly of poison, her stomach squirming. Her refusal had angered him. The next thrust of the spoon had cut her lower lip and released a trickle of blood.

Until then the seal across her mouth had robbed her of her voice. While alone she had tried to call out and had achieved only a thin, throaty squeal. Suddenly, with the hurt and the up-springing of new fear, she had blurted, "No, stop, *stop!*"

He had clamped a hand over her mouth so violently

that her head had struck the wall. Dazed, unable to breathe, she had wrenched herself free and yelled. At the highest pitch of her lungs she had cried out for help. Utterly blind to the coming blow, she could not possibly have avoided it. In his hair-trigger rage, he had brought his fist smashing across her jaw.

When she recovered he was gone. The strap was again stuck tightly across her swollen lips. A lump on the back of her head was throbbing. The taste of blood was in her mouth and fragments of broken teeth on her tongue.

The man with the hard-driving heels, the harsh hands, and the brutal fist—he was the one who was standing outside now.

There had been another moment when she had felt the cruelty of his hands—a moment of alarm.

It had happened early yesterday morning, she thought just before sunrise. Both of them had been here for perhaps an hour, ignoring her while keeping themselves busy with some sort of task, and something had startled them.

A noise she hadn't been able to hear? A dangerous approach? All she knew was that they had reacted swiftly to an emergency.

The rough one had sprung to her side and had closed both his hands around her throat—a warning desperately meant.

When clutching her, he had inadvertently dislodged the plug in her right ear. He had not been aware of this. The plug had not dropped out; it had stayed loosely in place and she had listened past it.

At first there had been nothing to hear except a lapping of water. She had held herself fearfully still. The rough one kneeling at her side had been motionless also, his hands hard and ready on her throat. The other—— She had not known whether or not he was still in the room. Her heart was a tumult, her skin cold with fear, and if the

30

door had been opened she had not felt it. After a moment she had heard the crunching sound of a man moving about on ground covered with gravel or crushed sea-shell. She had assumed that the rough one's partner had gone out to investigate. Next she had heard, outside, someone whistling softly a fragment of a tune.

Griff does that, she had thought. *Griff whistles to himself in just that same way.* That snatch of a tune—wasn't it one of his favourites? She was too panicky for clear recognition. Was it really Griff out there? Was he searching for her—and so close? If she could only call out to him—— *Griff! Griff!*

The threatening hands were ready to crush out instantly any sound she might make.

She must have given some sign she had heard. The rough one had noticed the loosened ear-plug. Freeing one hand for a second, he had crammed the wad back into place with a hard jab of his thumb. The whistling and the lapping of the water had vanished. The hands, both swiftly back on her throat, had tightened until her breath was almost stopped. She had lost awareness of everything except her own choking terror.

Then the rough one had abruptly left her, as if the other had pulled him off. The alarm had passed. She had stretched her neck to help relieve the constriction, drawing deep breaths. After more moments of wary stillness, both of them had quickly slipped away. Whatever had happened, it had been a close thing, dangerously close.

During her nightmarish periods of half sleep she had been haunted by the whistling. She thought of being at home with Griff, she busy in the kitchen, Griff working at something in his shop—it had been like that in a small, lost way.

But had it really been Griff? To judge from the length of time she had been in the boat, when they were bringing her here, this place must be far up the bay to the north of Belle Loma, or across the bay to the east, on Palmport Point. In both directions there were uninhabited sections of scrub pine and palmetto, with a few fishermen's shacks scattered along the water. Whichever it might be, where-ever she was, Griff would have had no reason to come. All his work was centred around Belle Loma, and he spent much of his spare time on Pelican Key.

Unless—— *Had* he been searching for her? No. No, because he had done nothing; he hadn't checked—whatever this building was—hadn't tried to enter. Either a co-incidence had brought him near, totally unaware of her whereabouts, or else it had been someone else, not Griff at all.

The whistling—Griff—Pelican Key—— It was the far-thest in the cluster of islands in the bay and the one place where they wouldn't have dared to take her. Griff's cottage, where he had lived before their marriage, overlooked the cove. He went there often, almost every day. Since their separation he had also spent the night there fre-quently—she had seen the far-away lights of the windows. There was a short stretch of beach, but Bill Rockwood's house sat above it, and Bill, living there all the year round, rarely left the island. These were the only accesses to it, and the only other structure on it was an unused shack back in the jungle. All the rest of the shore was an im-penetrable overgrowth of mangroves. They wouldn't have risked taking her there. Coming and going as they had, separately and together, they could not possibly have avoided being heard and seen by Bill and Griff.

No; this hiding-place could not be on Pelican Key. Griff had not been searching for her and his work would not have taken him to any other remote locality. It couldn't have been Griff she had heard. Perhaps, in her longing for him, for his strength and his love, she had imagined a resemblance in the whistling. That was the answer—her mind a swirling of pain and terror, she had imagined it.

As the rough one resumed walking, coming still nearer, the impulses communicated through the floor grew more complex. A second man was advancing quietly behind the first. When the first reached the door he stopped and waited there until the other joined him.

A movement of air across her face told her the door had been opened and closed. Invariably, as soon as they were inside, they came straight to her, carefully checked her bonds and made sure the ear-plugs were firmly in place. This time there was a new quality in their movements, an urgency. It quickened her heartbeat. They had come to a decision, to a time for action.

They drew away from her and for several minutes they were motionless at the door. Listening? . . . The air stirred as the door was opened again. The rough one hurried back and hooked his hands under her shoulders. He lifted her and pulled her along, her feet dragging. Once he had her outside the door, he stopped. A chilly breeze was blowing off the water. The second man bent his arms under her knees and they carried her.

She judged from their shiftings and turnings that they were taking her along a winding path. When they stopped again the man holding her legs stepped downward. The rough one followed to the same level, and they lowered her to a flooring. She smelled the characteristic odour compounded of gasoline and oil that meant a motor. This, and a gentle rocking told her they were aboard a boat. Immediately they covered her with something that felt coarse and stiff—a tarpaulin. It gave off a stale stink of fish.

For minute after minute there was no sound at all. The rocking of the boat increased and varied in its rhythm. It was adrift.

She turned her face aside, trying to escape the stench. She felt stifled by it and by a mingling of hope and dread, a life-or-death uncertainty. The one straw she could clutch was the thought that the uncertainty would not last much longer. Time was moving again, bringing her nearer to a culmination. The water all around her could be an avenue to long-lost comforts and safety. Or it could be utter finality. Here in the open darkness, unseen and unheard, they would find it a quick and easy task to lash an anchor to her body and drop her to the bottom of the bay.

They were allowing the boat to drift with the tidal current. Perhaps there was awakening activity along the waterfront nearby. At this time of the morning some of the skippers of the charter boats in the marinas would be making ready for the day's fishing, and others would already be putting out. No other craft were under way nearby—none she could hear—but for some reason the two men were painstakingly avoiding noise, guarding against every possibility of drawing attention to themselves.

When, finally, the engine was started, the man at the wheel kept it down to a low speed. The exhaust was a quiet unvarying vibration. The deck listed slightly; the boat was leaning into its course with its rudder to port. Heading into deeper water, it began to pitch. Before long the tilt of the deck changed towards the starboard side. She was noticing all this carefully. If they permitted her to live, and if she could remember these alterations——

Soon she became confused. They were slowly veering back and forth. Giving a wide berth to other boats riding at anchor? No; they kept it up until she was certain it was deliberate, and her confusion was hopeless.

After perhaps half an hour the deck came level and the pitching diminished. They were in shallow water again. The engine was switched off. Again the boat drifted, this time over a shorter distance. The two men, moving about, seemed to be pulling it in to a landing. The rasp-like vibration she felt could be the rubbing of a line across the toe-rail as it was being hauled in and made fast. The boat steadied to a slight rocking, and suddenly the tarpaulin was pulled off her.

She caught her breath as the rough one's hands hooked on to her again. By her arms and her knees she was lifted as before, then hoisted higher. For a moment she sat on a shelf-like edge while they climbed after her.

Their movements became quicker. They dragged her back from the edge, forced her down on her back, then hurried away. The engine was started at once, the throttle jerked up to a high notch. The exhaust snarled on a note of evil triumph as the boat sped out.

She lay still, listening to it until the sound passed beyond the reach of her hearing. The cold wind blew over her. Her finger-tips told her she was lying on weathered wood —spaced planks, a pier. There were scores of piers in and near Belle Loma. Had they actually brought her to one near her home? She began to sob quietly in her throat, and tears pooled on her closed eyelids. She could let herself believe she was almost back home again.

After a long time she felt the rapid, irregular tattoo of men running on to the pier. Suddenly hands were on her, kindly hands working at her bonds and the two strips adhering across her face. The strips left a rawness, as if some of her skin had torn away with them, but she scarcely felt it. The first blurred face she saw in the uncertain beam of a flashlight was Dick Carrick's. Then Tim Hampden's. Not her father's. Spencer Armstead was hugging her crushingly, his chin on her shoulder, choking out grateful sounds. She dug the plugs out of her ears. For the first time in an eon she heard her own voice, and it did not sound like her own.

"I want a bath!" She cried it out hysterically. "A bath, I want a long hot bath!"

Then she was on her feet and tottering towards a car, her father leading the way. With Dick supporting her on one side and Tim on the other, she was glorying in the simple freedom of her arms and legs. And she was wondering. *Griff—— Where is Griff? Why didn't Griff come?*

CHAPTER IV

IT WAS 4.40 a.m. when the four men came out of the police office. They divided themselves between the two unmarked sedans that had been waiting all night and started off in opposite directions, one car towards Gulf Boulevard, the other towards Belle Loma Way, quietly. Both turned to the north.

Chief of Police Teague left the office open behind him. Inside his own car, he snapped on the radio and sat for a moment, ordering himself to cool down. This was no time to get sore. He needed to keep a clear head, especially because he was still the only man on the force who knew what they were up against.

Teague had assumed all along that once the call from the Armstead home had finally buzzed in, the lid would be off. He and Dick Carrick together had mapped out their moves in detail; their plan of operations had been all set; they had simply been waiting for the starting gun. He had expected the message to be short and to the point. "She's here, let's go"—something like that would have been enough. Having kept himself bottled up so far, he had meant to tell his men immediately what was up and what to shoot for. But no. At the last minute Carrick—Spencer

36

Armstead rather, since Carrick was speaking for him—had rung in a change that would make the case tougher to handle and tougher still to crack.

"Nobody's to know Lynn was kidnapped," Carrick had said. Over Teague's protests he had insisted, "Absolutely nobody is to be let in on it, Dan! There's a damned good reason, a new angle, one that turned up just tonight. Potentially it's loaded with grief. If the news gets out now, before we've had time to dig, it'll probably play almighty hell later. The risk is too big."

To Teague's next question Carrick had answered, quickly breaking in, "Tell you about it next time I see you."

Teague had insisted. "I'll come up right now."

"No, don't, not yet. We want to get Lynn's story first. So far she's been able to tell us only a little. Doc Elder is with her now and won't let us question her until she's had some rest. You'll want to be in on that, of course—I'll let you know when. Meanwhile, Dan, not a word to anybody, understand? Otherwise take it the same way we had it."

Teague sank the ignition key and twisted its neck. "Otherwise" meant that he had had to send his men out to do a job under an imposed ignorance of what the job was. He couldn't fairly be expected to get results that way. But would Spencer Armstead expect him to get results anyhow? Damn right he would. And if results were not forthcoming in a hurry, what would Spencer Armstead do about it? Spencer Armstead would begin throwing his weight around even more.

Starting off, Teague gave himself another order: *Let's be fair about this.* His decision to co-operate fully had been of his own making. His reason behind it had been the same as Lynn's father's. Suppose he hadn't submitted to all Spencer Armstead's demands—then, if he had made a

37

wrong move and if, as a consequence, the kidnappers had killed Lynn—— The thought still brought him a shudder.

But it was difficult now. The danger to Lynn was past. So what had come up, why was this thing still so touchy and so risky? With Lynn back home, who could get hurt except the snatchers? . . . No matter—until he found out what Carrick's new angle was, he'd have to go on obeying commands from on high.

Teague turned his car southwards. On his right the Gulf was unlimited emptiness. He looked along the cross streets on his left, one after another, as he passed them. He saw what he expected to see, familiar cars parked under the pines, houses all dark, a respectable little community sound asleep.

What really burned him was the fact that he hadn't given his men a fair shake. He had first told them frankly that for reasons he couldn't explain he couldn't take them into his confidence until the break actually came—which in itself was no way to treat responsible officers. Then, when Carrick's call had finally come, he had hedged, which was worse. "Check anything of a suspicious nature"—he had had to leave it at that, well aware that this turned his resourceful, thinking team into so many aimless gropers. So now they were scouting the streets and watching the causeway without knowing what they were looking for.

At the point of the island, where the boulevard U turned into Belle Loma Way, everything was equally quiet until a familiar churning noise began shaking the sky towards the south-west. As it grew louder Teague put his head out of the window and saw lights skimming low over the bay. That helicopter was another part of Carrick's prearrangements. Out there at the Coast Guard base on Belmore Key, Carrick's friend Bob Sage, the commander, had also been losing sleep while waiting for an alert. The boys in the whirlybird had instructions to watch any and all marine activity, particularly to look for a motor-boat that might be heading up or down the coast at full speed. But like his own men, Teague thought wryly, they wouldn't know why.

Turning north now, he began taking particular interest in the piers along the bay front. There in a row of small houses on the water was the one Griff had rented. Griff hadn't stayed around the place very much since his break-up with Lynn, but he was at home now—at least his truck, his sedan, and his boat *Lotus* were all there. Teague noted this in passing; he was looking for a different boat, *Playgirl*, belonging to an offbeat character named Alec Poole.

What Teague knew about Poole wasn't too much or too good. He was unmarried, about thirty-five, lived some-where near Sarasota and spent his time ranging up and down this stretch of the Gulf Coast. Once or twice a year he breezed into Belle Loma and stayed a week or two, mostly hanging around the yacht club. He had no visible means of support except playing bridge and poker for stiff stakes, and an occasional fishing party on the *Playgirl*, for which he wasn't licensed. Irresponsible, allergic to work, and a scrounger. That was why Poole was always on the move, Teague thought—when the pickings grew thin and his welcome was worn out, he shoved off.

Poole was also a heavy drinker and unpredictable when drunk. He might turn pugnacious, or be uproariously happy, or sometimes morosely preoccupied. Teague had found him sleeping it off in various odd places—on a pub-lic bench, in a stranger's car, and once on the sea wall, where a roll in the wrong direction might have dropped him to the submerged rocks below. Teague was checking every pier from the point of Belle Loma northwards be-cause he might find *Playgirl* tied up anywhere it shouldn't be—Poole was that kind.

He had a woman who kept tagging around after him. Her name was Vina Something. Every time, soon after Poole had put in in his boat, the girl followed in her big convertible. Teague had heard that Poole often took off without telling her where he was bound, and then she'd go hunting for him. She was a short-haired redhead, attractive in a way that combined a childlike quality with hardness. Evidently she had an income of her own; she didn't seem to mind buying his drinks when they were bar-hopping together, or paying some of his bills. She even seemed to like the way he mistreated her at times and the vagrant life he led her. Maybe that was true love, or maybe she just didn't know what was good for her, or didn't care. Anyhow Teague had asked a few quiet questions and found out that on this jaunt they were staying at the Azalea Motel.

Teague had no logical reason to think of Poole in connection with the snatch. He hadn't been keeping an eye on Poole—Spencer Armstead would have had none of that—only keeping him in mind. But having no better lead—so far the radio hadn't let out a peep from either of the other two cars—he simply thought it might not be a bad idea to check on Alec Poole first.

It was just ahead, its big neon sign still shining: *Gulf Swimming—Bay Fishing—TV—Air Cond—Vacancy—AZA-LEA MOTEL.*

As the helicopter circled over the bay Alec Poole watched its lights with a derisive grin. He was slouched in a canvas chair in the cockpit of *Playgirl*, his legs stretched out, a pint bottle of bourbon in his left hand. For more than half an hour, since quietly bringing his express cruiser into the dock, he had been lolling here, relaxing in the cool dawn breeze and feeling good.

The strain, the tightrope walking, the day-and-night

vigilance, the constant fear that something might slip—all that had been a real sweat, but now it was almost over. They had pulled off the toughest part according to plan. There had been a bad break at the beginning, while they were grabbing the Armstead girl, and a narrow squeak later, when they might have been found right there in the hide-out with her, but otherwise there had been no serious hitches.

Alec Poole gazed up at the approaching helicopter with his grin growing. Ah, he felt good, very good and very confident. The rest would be comparatively easy, much smoother sailing. They had outsmarted the cops in advance by taking pains to think of small details from a cop's viewpoint. In order to cut off every possible lead they had checked and double checked back and forth until they were certain they hadn't left the slightest trace.

The tarpaulin, for example, as unlikely a clue as it might have been—Poole had lifted it off a docked shrimp-boat when no one was about, and after using it they had simply chucked it overboard. The money, divided into two equal bundles, was cached in a place where no one would dream of looking. The town cops and the Coast Guardsmen could sniff around for that money until they were dizzy—it was going to be slipped right past their noses in a way they would never suspect. That would be the next move and there wasn't any hurry about it. Poole would simply laze around as usual until the opening presented itself. Afterwards he would go his separate way, entirely in the clear and—brother—loaded.

The helicopter had swung inshore and was tracing the water-front with its searchlight. Poole made no move to get himself out of sight. When it was about to pass overhead he sagged lower in the chair and closed his eyes, simulating sleep.

The flapping noise beat down on him, and the light

glared redly through his lids. It hovered a moment. After it had flown on, Poole dropped the pretence, took a pull from the bottle, and laughed at it. They were reporting him by radio to the Coast Guard base on Belmore Key, of course. "Check on a man in a boat at the pier of the Azalea Motel"—something of the sort. Poole was far from worried. Those guys in the chopper didn't realize it, but they had been baited into helping him set up an alibi.

Poole drank again and began glancing towards the highway beyond the motel. Within a few minutes, he expected, he'd be having a visitor or two aboard the *Playgirl*.

The neon sign sent its glow over the pier so that Poole could read his wrist-watch. Almost five. He pinched out the stem and turned the hands backward to—he figured for a moment—about one-forty would be right. He had taken the boat out at eleven, telling Vina as she was going to bed that he wanted to run down to the yacht club for a couple of nightcaps. He had actually done that. He hadn't left until the bar closed at one. He had taken the pint away with him and had left it capped until half an hour ago.

Having set his watch back, he leaned down and struck it sharply against the deck. Fragments of the shattered crystal fell out. Poole made sure the watch had stopped, reflecting that although this was by no means a new trick, the situation as a whole would make it a convincing one.

Looking up quickly, he saw a car stopping in the multi-coloured shine of the motel sign. Painted in foot-high letters on its side was the word POLICE. Well!—the chief himself. Company had come faster than Poole had counted on, but it didn't matter.

He quietly overturned his chair sidewards and arranged himself in a sprawl on the deck. Tilting the bottle, he dribbled some of the whisky on his shirt, then bent his left arm so that his wrist lay near the broken pieces of watch

42

crystal and let the rest of the whisky spill out. It was really a good break for him that it was Dan Teague who was coming; this could present the chief with a fairly familiar picture.

He lay still, listening. Teague was walking forward past the guests' parked cars. He came the length of the pier, stopped, and turned on his flashlight. Poole heard him give a grunt of disappointment and disgust.

Teague came aboard and stooped for a closer look, paying particular attention to the wrist-watch. Teague said "Hmpf" again, turned, and ducked into the cabin.

Not stirring, Poole heard the chief poking about, opening and closing lockers, then the icebox, even looking into the head. After a moment of quiet Poole opened his eyes a slit. The chief was turning from one of the bunks, leaving it rumpled, and now he began feeling under the pillow and the mattress of the other. Having found nothing at all, he came back on deck, stepped over Poole, and looked into the lazarette. Poole was having a hard time keeping a grin down, but he managed.

Teague shook his shoulder. "Poole. . . . Poole!"

He mumbled, "Lemme 'lone."

A harder shake. "Wake up! Mind if I take a look around this boat?"

"Whum?" Since he had already searched it, what was the point of asking now? A matter of procedure, probably, or a test. Poole opened his eyes, seeming to drag the lids up, and squinted painfully in the dazzle of the flashlight. "Who zat?"

"Dan Teague. Making a routine check."

"A whuh?"

"Just checking. Okay?"

"Sure, sure, he'p y'rself."

Poole relapsed into apparent unconsciousness with a feeling that given half a provocation Teague might have kicked him. Without bothering to repeat his search, the chief pulled himself up to the pier and walked back to the front of the motel. He didn't go as far as his car, but stopped at the door of the office. He was ringing the night bell. After a wait of several minutes Poole heard Teague saying, "One of your guests didn't quite make it, Mr. Clane."

Both Teague and Clane came to the edge of the pier. Again Poole lay motionless in the spot of the flashlight.

"Can't say it amazes me," Clane commented.

"What time did he pull in?"

"Didn't hear him, chief. A motel-keeper doesn't get much sleep most nights, but some nights he's luckier, like this one."

"Well, then, did you happen to notice when he put out?"

"About eleven. His girl's room's near the office, and I heard him telling her he was going down to the yacht club."

"Driving's easier, so why didn't he use his girl's car?"

"Maybe he figures a boat's safer on the way back, as potted as he gets himself. Doesn't like cars anyway. Says a car is nothing but a bunch of nuts and bolts, but a boat's like a woman, has a personality all her own. We better not leave him out here, chief. Might rain."

They came aboard, grasped Poole's arms, and pulled him up to his knees. Poole purposely made it an exasperating task. By the time they had lifted him to the pier both of them were muttering about damn drunks. He stayed rubbery, letting his head roll and his feet drag, while they wrestled him to the door of his room, then inside, and flopped him on to the bed.

"Want to ask you something, Mr. Clane. Has this man been behaving in any unusual way these past few days?"

44

"He sure has," Clane answered. "He behaves unusual all the time."

"I mean—suspicious."

"Hard to say. In and out at all hours, but for him that's normal. You got something special in mind, chief?"

"Mr. Clane, would you do me a small favour? I could get a search warrant, but this way it'll be quicker. Would you just dig around in that suitcase while I watch, then look into those dresser drawers?"

"Well—— He sure won't catch me at it. Considering who's asking——"

Poole remained inert on the bed. There were small noises at the suitcase, then the sliding sound of the drawers, in and out. Teague said, "Well, that does it," and they returned to the door.

After the latch clicked Poole turned on his back and lay listening with a puzzled frown. Teague wasn't overlooking any bets; now he was doing something else outside. Poole left the bed and peered through the almost-closed slats of the venetian blind.

The chief was opening the trunk of Vina's convertible. So she'd forgotten again and left the key in the ignition lock? Poole couldn't help snorting. That trunk was always piled full of Vina's junk—picnic hamper, beach umbrella, old shoes, wet swim-suits, towels, lord knew what else, all in a tangle. It would keep Teague busy for minutes, and it did, with Clane watching and wagging his head over the mess.

Teague closed the trunk, returned the key to the ignition lock, then signalled Clane to accompany him to Vina's door. He knocked loudly until Vina came. As they entered Vina's room Poole returned to the bed.

Minutes later he heard them leaving. Clane went back into the office and Teague trudged on to his car. As soon as the car was gone Vina's door opened again. Her bare feet padded across to Poole's. She came in and snapped the light-switch.

"Alec! What was that about?"

He lifted his head. She was wearing a thin shortie nightgown. Her red hair was rumpled. She looked as cute as she always did when she was blistering mad. "Mmm?" he said.

She came closer. "That cop wanting to search my room. Why?"

"You been running any rum lately, baby?"

"Comedian! Alec? You been up to something? Cop snooping around!"

"Did you let him?"

"Why not? I've got nothing to hide." She knew why he smiled at that, but she didn't smile back. "I said okay just to get rid of 'em. What did he think he'd find?"

Poole swung his feet to the floor and ambled towards her. "Wouldn't know, sugar. Forget it. Go back to bed."

"I'm wide awake." She put her arms around him and pressed her head to his chest. "You worry me so, Alec."

"Forget it, I said." He pulled her arms loose and pushed her towards the door. "I'm bushed. Go on now, baby, beat it."

When she was reluctantly gone, he found a fresh bottle in the dresser and switched off the lamps. He sat on the edge of the bed, drinking and chuckling to himself. It had gone even better than he had hoped. Just one more move to make now, in Poole's own good time, and the whole deal would be sweetly polished off.

For no particular reason Dan Teague was driving towards Fargo Causeway, which crossed the bay to lead directly into the central street of Palmport. He expected his men stationed there to have nothing worth reporting.

The helicopter was still flapping around over the bay on its own wild goose chase.

Teague was glumly discouraged. Alec Poole, his only lead, a thin hope at best, had petered out. Dick Carrick's "new angle", whatever it was, had better begin building up into something solid. So far there was nothing else.

CHAPTER V

DR. BERTRAM ELDER, finishing the examination, summed up his findings with a well-satisfied "Ah-*ha!*" and smoothed the sheet across Lynn's shoulders. A grey bear of a man, he had been unhurried, orderly, and gentle. Lynn had submitted drowsily under the lingering effects of the injection he had given her during his first call before dawn this morning. It was late afternoon now—she had had almost twelve hours of uninterrupted sleep.

"All okay, Dr. Bert?"

"The bounce of youth," he said. "It never ceases to amaze me. You make me feel very old."

She stretched herself blissfully, smiling up at him. "Oh, wonderful, being able to do that."

"Hungry?"

"Starving!"

"Your father's preparing a tray for you now." He turned to close his medicine case. "You're a tough-fibred young woman, Lynn, but be careful and don't overdo. This has been more of a shock to you than you may realize, so take it easy for a few—— Here, what's this?"

"I'm getting up," Lynn said. "Getting up under my own power. It's the first time this week—feels like the first in years. I'm going to soak in a hot tub again. Then I'm going to put on clean clothes. You wouldn't believe how much I'm going to enjoy myself just moving around."

"Hmm. Well—— I suggest postponing the soak. Those men downstairs are waiting to hear—— Ah-ha! See?"

Her knees had buckled and he had caught her arms. She leaned against him and steadied herself.

"I'm okay now."

"Not entirely, you're not. Get dressed if you like, but you're to stay right here in this room until you've had something to eat and feel stronger."

"I will."

"They'll be coming up in a few minutes, but don't let them tire you with their questions."

"I won't."

"Lynn——"

"Yes, Dr. Bert?"

"Have you told Griff——?"

She shook her head. "Nobody."

"Isn't it time you did?"

"Not yet."

"Well, it's the sort of secret a woman can't keep for very long, you know, even if she wants to." Immediately after leaving Griff she had learned she was pregnant. "Telling him would certainly help to straighten out this foolishment between you two."

"Not really. It wouldn't really fix anything. It would bring us back together for the wrong reason."

"Reason my hat! What's reason got to do with it? You love him, you belong with him, just as he loves and belongs with you. Go back to him, Lynn."

"You know how much I want that. I'm sure of myself now. All the mistakes I made—I won't make them again. But it won't work until Griff gets himself straightened out too. That's something nobody else can do for him, and

48

because he's Griff it won't come easy." She shook her head again. "I know what I mean, but it's terribly hard to explain. And it mustn't be forced."

"I feel not only old," the doctor muttered, "but incompetent too."

She smiled and kissed his cheek. As she moved to the wardrobe closet, weaving a little, he waited, and when she had safely made it he left the bedroom.

On the stairs he met Spencer Armstead coming up. Lynn's father was carrying a loaded breakfast-tray covered with spread napkins. Although he had slept through part of the morning, he still looked haggard with strain.

"She's entirely all right, Bert?"

"As I told you before, Spence, yes. Lynn has come through it in better shape than you have." Dr. Elder asked sternly, "What's wrong with you now? Why haven't you stopped worrying?"

"It's not over yet, not by a long shot." "This outrage", as Spencer Armstead invariably termed it, had turned him into a vengeful man. "Are you absolutely sure she— wasn't——?"

"Spence, I assured you of that this morning, and she has confirmed it. No, she wasn't raped. The blow didn't break her jaw. The swelling will be there for a few days, but it's only a bruise, and there's no rush about the dental work. Best thing right now is to get that food in her. And, Spence"—as Lynn's father started past—"she asked about Hal first thing, both visits. I said he's coming along all right. Better to avoid upsetting her with that just now. Actually Hal's condition is worse—he's not holding his own."

At that Spencer Armstead's face took on a stricken look. He said, "I'll keep it from her until she's stronger." Seeming fearful and at a loss, he turned away again; but again the doctor stopped him.

"Spence, aren't you being unfair to Griff about this? I think he deserves to be told what——"

"No! Absolutely not!"

Dr. Elder stood alone on the stairs a moment, puzzled and shocked by the vehemence of Spencer Armstead's answer.

Stopping in the living-room, Bertram Elder had interrupted a conference. Chief of Police Dan Teague was there with Dick Carrick and Tim Hampden. The doctor had given them the same assurances he had given Lynn's father and had asked them to wait ten or fifteen minutes before going up. After warning them not to press her too hard, he had left the house. Now Carrick resumed.

"There you have it, Dan. This snatch wasn't pulled by professional hoodlums. All the signs say the case is localized in and around Belle Loma. It was a damned smart job, and in order to bring it off they had to know their way around in the dark better than the average resident does."

Teague envied Carrick his self-assurance. It came of experience. In Teague's fifteen years as a police officer he had never before tackled a kidnapping case. Carrick had, some years ago, while working out of the Miami office of the FBI—a major one.

"They haven't made a run for it, as far as we know," Carrick went on, "so they're still here in town or somewhere nearby, and the money is probably hidden just as close to home. An all-out, big-scale investigation is unnecessary. The area is small, the possibilities limited."

Teague nodded, conceding the logic of the point. The reports coming from outside Belle Loma had been consistently negative. The State Highway Patrol, the Coast Guard, the inspectors at the many road-blocks who were stopping all cars in an effort to contain the recent infestation of the Mediterranean fruit-fly—nothing from any of them. Inside Belle Loma as well, the chief's men had wound up the night shrugging their shoulders. Teague himself had turned up here with a big zero. Running down his only lead to the last doubt, he had checked on Alec Poole at the yacht club, and with that it had fizzled out altogether.

"We'll get faster results," Carrick went on, "by working at it privately and quietly from the inside. In fact, we have no choice."

Teague knew why the FBI couldn't come in. The United States mail had not been used. Thanks to their geographical location there was no possibility that a state line had been crossed—the nearest was three hundred miles to the north. A federal law permitted this to be presumed after seven days, but Lynn had been returned after only three days, almost to the hour. A new law was coming before Congress to reduce the waiting period to twenty-four hours, but it was not yet in effect. Had the snatchers taken advantage of all this? Teague thought so—almost certainly they had deliberately planned it so as to keep the FBI out. And did this imply special knowledge? No—the information had been printed many times in the papers and news magazines.

"We'll handle it in such a way," Tim Hampden was adding, "that Griff won't know we suspect him."

"Griff——" Teague rubbed his bristly head. "I just can't believe it of Griff."

"Naturally, Dan, it's hard for you to accept the possibility," Carrick said. "I don't like it either. I admit it hadn't occurred to me until last night, and when it did it gave me a bad jolt. But there it is, a possibility very definitely. We have to face it."

"I like it even less than either of you," Tim Hampden put in, "—thinking it was Griff who did that to Hal, or

51

helped to do it. But so far it's the only possibility we have to work on."

"We have to stick with it, Dan," Carrick said. "Lynn's story may give us other leads, but nothing she might say will throw this one out."

Teague frowned at them. "You seem to be going into this with a fixed idea that Griff's guilty."

"Certainly not!" Carrick was offended. "Never look at a case in the light of a preconceived theory—that's basic. In this one we can't be too careful. We all appreciate how explosive it is. No, Dan; we'll have to be as careful as possible of our facts, particularly if they point to Griff. Certainly we'll have to dig for more evidence, all of us, and, whatever we may find, evaluate it with open minds."

"But your reason for suspecting Griff——" Teague insisted. "Just because he showed up here last night for the first time in months——"

"Last night of all nights, Dan. And he did it not just once but three times. I haven't told you about the other two. The first was early in the evening, when Spence was here alone. He happened to see Griff through that picture window." Carrick pointed and Teague looked at the island-studded bay beyond. "It was getting dark. Griff was in his boat, close inshore. He'd cut the motor and was drifting past. Spence said he was pretending to be busy with a snarled line but actually he was giving this place a good looking-over."

"Why not, if he wanted to see Lynn," Teague asked, "and was hoping to make it sort of accidental?"

"Possibly," Carrick went on. "The second time was between eleven-thirty and midnight. By then Tim and I had been waiting here with Spence for hours. I went outside to look around the grounds, and as I came through the patio from the bayside door I saw a pair of headlights turning at the corner—crawling. There seemed to be something stealthy about it, so I watched.

"It was Griff in his pick-up truck. He was leaning over the steering-wheel and peering at this house. He eased past, as if trying to avoid attracting attention, then picked up speed and swung out of sight at the next corner. I thought it was damned peculiar, the way Griff had shown a special interest in this place twice within a few hours on the very night when we were expecting a final message from the kidnappers."

"So then he dropped back later, came in, and asked questions," Teague said. "He stopped in my office next and asked more questions. You think all this shows guilty knowledge. I think—well, wanting to see Lynn, he was anxious and hesitant both."

"Possibly," Carrick said again. "But there's another circumstance I haven't told you about, Dan. It's much stronger. On the basis of that one point alone Spence is convinced—but of course he's prejudiced."

"So am I, but in the opposite direction," Teague retorted. "I know it's the wrong attitude, but it's going to take plenty of proof to make me believe Griff had a hand in this."

"All right, Dan. Before telling you about that one thing, and before talking to Lynn, let's see what we have without it."

"Sure, let's."

Teague rose, feeling he ought to get a firmer grip on the reins. He respected Carrick's training and experience as an investigator, but Carrick had no official status now—and after all, who was the chief of police here anyhow?

"I was in early, even before Mr. Armstead knew Lynn had been kidnapped, so let's go back to the scene." Pulled out of bed by the news, Teague had arrived while the ambulance was still there. "No witnesses. No footprints, no tyre-tracks—if there had been any, the rain washed them out. No dropped clues. No sign of the weapon that was used on Hal, if there was one. Lynn's car was left there where she'd parked it, not touched. They got her away in some other car and we don't know whose. Where it went from there—not a sign. That's the start, then—a big blank."

Carrick nodded. Teague turned to the collection of evidence arranged on the desk beside the tape recorder.

"First, these notes——"

The two ransom notes were each enclosed in a cellophane envelope. They were composed of printed words in various sizes of type which had been cut out of newspapers. The cut edges were straight; evidently a razor blade had been used. The words were pasted on the commonest type of sulphite typewriter paper, obtainable at any sundries store or stationer's, and impossible to trace. In Teague's presence Carrick had attempted to develop latent fingerprints on the paper and had found none except Spencer Armstead's. Rubber gloves or tweezers, Teague had thought. If these notes indicated anything at all, it was a very slick operator. The man who had put them together had painstakingly robbed them of all value as evidence.

"They don't point to Griff or anybody else," Teague said.

"That's right," Carrick agreed.

An empty soft-drink bottle sat on the desk. It had contained the second note. During the second night it had been tossed over the sea wall, manifestly from a boat drifting past. There had been no sound of a motor, or of the bottle landing in the grass, and it hadn't been found until after daylight. Again, no fingerprints. Again, no possibility of tracing this particular bottle. Others exactly like it were stacked by the caseful behind every lunch counter and in every food market on the beaches.

"No good at all," Teague said.

"Right," from Carrick.

There were several items here which Teague hadn't seen before—a tangle of cloth tape and two small irregular lumps of a substance which Teague couldn't name off-hand.

"Where'd this stuff come from?"

"Brought it with me from the Peterson pier this morning," Carrick explained.

The Peterson pier, Teague had learned through Carrick's phone call early this morning, was where the snatchers had left Lynn. After checking on Alec Poole and getting nowhere there, Teague had had a look at it. The Peterson house sat at the tip end of a finger fill in the bay —a long projection of man-made land dredged from the bay bottom, sea-walled and platted for home sites. Construction on the house had been suspended when it was not quite completed. Other houses nearby sat in various stages of construction, untouched for months, because of litigation among the developers. Pending a settlement, the road leading into it was barricaded and it was plentifully posted with *Keep Out* and *No Trespassing* signs. The project seemed to be jinxed, but the lay-out had served the kidnappers' purpose perfectly—an isolated point of land, the pier of an empty house, nobody living nearby. After examining the pier, Teague had come away empty-handed—Carrick had already been there.

"This is what they used on Lynn's wrists and ankles, Dan. Ordinary masking tape. Get it at any hardware store. Unusually wide, but that detail probably won't help." Carrick had the two small lumps in his fingers. "Wax-impregnated cotton. Anti-noise ear-stopples sold under a brand name in most drugstores." He was looking hard at Teague.

"Ear-stopples!" Teague exclaimed. "What didn't they

want her to hear?" Realizing it was the question that Carrick had led him to ask, he added quickly, "I'll answer that. Probably their voices. Maybe certain noises inside the hide-out or nearby. Or"—he finished it reluctantly—"or maybe she would have *recognized* their voices."

"The last seems the likeliest," Carrick said, "—that she knows, and knows well, one or the other of the men, or even both."

"So? Lynn knows a lot of men." This bothered Teague regardless. "A lot of men besides Griff. Why? Why would *he* do such a thing to his own wife?"

"Spence can answer that better than I can, Dan." Carrick asked quietly, "Have you noticed Griff acting suspiciously these past days?"

"After work he wanders around a lot, at all hours," Teague said levelly. "You know what I suspect him of because of that? I strongly suspect him of feeling damned lonely."

Carrick persisted. "Otherwise?"

"No."

"You'll be keeping an eye on him now? In a way that won't put him on his guard?"

"That's my job."

Carrick nodded. "His house should be searched, but without his knowledge. You can't do it legally without a warrant, Dan, and getting one would tip our hand. Lynn still has a key, probably. She can go in while Griff's out, with one or two of us to witness. Then there's his other place over on Pelican Key."

"He never leaves it locked," Teague said, feeling his face flushing. "Drop in any time."

"One other thing." Carrick was entirely unruffled. "Lynn has no idea we have reason to suspect Griff. Spence understood he wasn't to mention it. We'll hear her through before telling her. Handling it in that way, we'll get it straight, without any tendency on her part to colour her story either for or against him. Do you agree, Dan?"

Handling it in that way, they might make a dupe of Lynn—lead her unwittingly into a statement incriminating her husband.

"Let's go," Teague said shortly, hating his own inescapable part in it.

Carrick led the way up the stairs, carrying the tape recorder. Tim Hampden took along the ransom notes. Following them, Teague remembered now that Carrick somehow hadn't got around to telling him about that certain circumstance which had already convicted Griff in Spencer Armstead's mind.

CHAPTER VI

She had just finished phoning an aircraft flash to the Miami Filter Centre, Lynn told them, when Wilmer Frost came into the shelter to take over the 4–8 a.m. watch. She remembered logging the report at 3.52. There was the usual exchange between them—"How's business tonight?" and "Slow, only eight planes since midnight, mostly jet bombers." She went down the stairs from the roof to the top floor of the bank building where the night watchman was holding the elevator for her. In the usual way he took her down to the lobby and unlocked the entrance to let her out, and she walked around the corner into the side street where she had left her convertible parked. Two or three other cars were lined up there, but that wasn't unusual and she didn't give them any particular notice. The two men may have been crouching behind one of them, or hiding in the alley behind the building—she didn't know.

She opened the driver's door, put her handbag on the seat, and was cranking the window down, about to slide in, when she heard the swift footfalls of the men rushing at her from behind. It startled and froze her, and she had time only to turn her head before they were on her. The light of the street lamp was in her eyes, and she glimpsed them only as two fast-moving figures without any recognizable features.

The first grabbed her, pulled her out, and crushed her against his body with one arm, pinioning both of hers. As he brought his other hand upward to her face she saw it as white—gloved. The cloth glove was cold, wet—saturated with a volatile liquid. It pressed hard over her mouth and nostrils and she tried to shut out the fumes, but in her grasping struggle to tear free she could not help herself.

The stuff—not ether or chloroform, but something else vaguely familiar—did not have a quick effect. She squirmed and kicked her heels at her captor's legs until the second man grabbed and lifted her ankles. As he straightened she got a blurred look at him. He had eyes, shadowed eyes, but no face. His whole head was hidden inside a shoulder-length black hood.

They carried her, hurrying, and began forcing her through the rear door of a dark-coloured sedan. At that point a sudden mischance threatened to disrupt their whole plan.

A car, appearing at the corner, turned into the side street. Its headlight beams swept over them. Lynn heard a low shout of alarm and recognized the voice of Hal Hampden. The car slid to a screaking stop. Hal sprang out and began running towards them.

One of the two men tore away from Lynn. She heard the sounds of blows. Still struggling, although the fumes were beginning to numb her senses, she was able to twist herself about. She saw Hal lying in the street in the flare of the headlights. The hooded man, crouched, had one hand clutched on Hal's throat, the other in Hal's hair; he was smashing Hal's head savagely against the kerbstone. He sprang up, kicked Hal with brutal force twice, then rushed back.

The man holding Lynn blurted in a hoarse whisper, "You dirty fool!"

The other snapped, "Shut up!"

The next moments were out of focus in Lynn's memory. Now her strength was failing; the two men overpowered her easily. She found herself inside the sedan, held helpless by one of them while the other took the wheel. The motor whirred and the sedan spurted off.

The man clutching Lynn blurted, "God's sake, don't, don't!"

"*Shut up!*"

She stared in horror and felt the car lurch twice, violently, as the driver ran both right wheels over Hal's body.

So far they had not interrupted her. She had her legs curled under her on the chaise-longue in a corner of her bedroom. Spencer Armstead sat close beside her, his face ruddy with sustained anger. Dan Teague and Dick Carrick, both standing, had listened searchingly. Tim Hampden was sitting on the edge of the bed, his shoulders slumped, looking heavy-hearted.

"I'm sorry, Tim."

"I don't understand it. How did Hal happen to turn up when he did?" Hampden openly resented that trick of circumstances. "He's a night owl, I know that, and once a party starts him off he keeps on going, he never wants to turn in. But—— Did he know when you'd be coming off duty?"

"Of course. Hal has dropped in at the post several Sunday nights on his way home, just to visit with me, and other times I've found him waiting for me in the street. Those men couldn't have known he liked to do that. He caught them when they were least expecting it. If only he hadn't been alone! He isn't a slugger—he was no match for such a brute."

"But seeing them grabbing you—— It wouldn't have mattered to Hal if there had been four or five of them." Hampden wagged his head. "A crazy, hopeless thing! He couldn't help doing it and it did nobody any good. Makes me sick to think that if he'd come a minute or two later it wouldn't have happened to him at all, and you would have been no worse off either."

Hampden's bitterness brought an uncomfortable silence. Lynn felt pressure in him. Did he mean to say more—that Lynn, still married to Griff, should have discouraged these early-morning visits of Hal's and other dates as well—that, because she hadn't, she was to blame? But if he thought that, he held it in; he shook his head again, hopelessly, and looked away.

Lynn turned her eyes curiously to Dick Carrick and Dan Teague. Something in Carrick's attitude had disturbed her—a kind of caginess. Teague, listening so carefully, seemed apprehensive. She couldn't guess why and it was making her uneasy.

"Shall I go on?"

"A few questions first, Lynn," Carrick suggested. "When they spoke, there in the car, did you recognize their voices?"

"Those short, hoarse whispers? They were in a panic and probably didn't sound like themselves anyhow. I was so scared and so dizzy from breathing the fumes—— Later I realized what that stuff was, Dick. Cleaning fluid."

"Carbon tet. It works very much like ether." Carrick and Teague exchanged glances. Carbon tetrachloride bottled as dry-cleaning fluid under several brand names
60

was even more widely available than masking tape and cheap sulphite paper. "Did it put you all the way out?"

"It took the fight out of me all right, but I knew in a foggy way what was happening. I was still in the car when they strapped me up. Then they stopped somewhere and carried me to a motor-boat, and when——"

"The boat, Lynn," Carrick interrupted. "Was there anything familiar about it, or recognizable? The sound of the exhaust, or the way it rode?" When she shook her head: "A cabin cruiser? Did they put you inside a cabin?"

"No, on the open deck, to judge from the wind. Coming back, they covered me with a tarpaulin that smelled of fish. But going, they didn't. Then, when we got to where-ever it was they took me, they carried me again and——" Lynn paused. "*There's* something I hadn't thought of be-fore. Later, when they took me out of the place to bring me back, they seemed to be lugging me along a winding path. But that first night, when they took me in, it didn't twist at all—it was short and straight."

At the mention of the winding path Dan Teague had stirred and frowned, as if it had brought an unwelcome association of ideas. He asked quickly, "Can you be sure of that, Lynn, as drugged as you were?"

"It may not seem to make sense, but it *was* like that— short and straight going in, long and winding coming out." She puzzled over it a moment, then insisted, "I *do* remember, because—— Before taking me inside the place, they put me down on the ground for a few minutes, then went in and used a deodorant spray."

Startled, Carrick grasped at that. "A deodorant spray?"

"Some sort of air freshener, as it's called," Lynn said. "Every single time when they came in, they used the spray. It smelled awful, like the cheapest sort of perfume. They doused it around until it was so strong I almost gagged. It got on my dress and in my hair, so that I

61

couldn't smell anything else for hours afterwards. It was so sickening that when they tried to feed me I couldn't eat."

"But you did eat later?"

"I told you this morning why one of them hit me—the same one who was so brutal to Hal. After that he wasn't taking any more chances—he didn't care whether I starved. When the other one offered food I could manage a little. I'm not sure what it was, because of that awful perfume. Pork and beans, I think. Cold, probably right out of the can."

"Why do you think they used the spray, Lynn?" Carrick asked. "Because the place has a characteristic smell of its own, one that would help you to identify it later? Between times, when the scent began wearing off, did the background smell ever come through?"

"It never wore off entirely," Lynn said, wrinkling her nose. "I can still smell it." She turned her gaze on her father. "Dad, this isn't all one-sided. I want to know what happened to you too. When did you find out?"

"Monday morning. Something wakened me earlier than usual, a feeling that something was wrong. It was about six-thirty. I looked into this room and your bed hadn't been touched. I went downstairs and your car wasn't here. I was picking up the phone, about to call the Ground Observer post, when I saw a folded sheet of paper slipped under the front door." Spencer Armstead's face darkened at the recollection. He waved a hand towards Carrick.

"Spence called me and I came right over." Carrick was bringing the first ransom note towards Lynn. "This warned him not to notify the police, and for your sake he was determined to do exactly as they demanded. We went out looking for your car, wherever it was, because it might raise questions. We found it still parked beside the

62

bank building. I was going to drive it back. But Dan was there. He'd already checked at the GOC post and had been told you'd left at four, and he wanted to know what about that."

Teague said, "At first they wouldn't tell me one thing about what had happened to you. Hal had been found about an hour earlier. Tim had been notified, and Hal was in the operating-room by then, but Mr. Armstead and Dick knew nothing about it. Warning or no warning, this was too serious—they couldn't hold out on me. I agreed to go along with Mr. Armstead all the way—to sit still and keep it strictly to myself until they'd done everything possible to get you safely back home."

Lynn was gazing wide-eyed at the ransom note inside the transparent envelope. "Two hundred thousand dollars! Dad, did you actually pay them two hundred thousand dollars?"

"I had no choice, Lynn dear. It took my last cent and even that wasn't enough. I had to dig into your funds too." He was referring to the substantial bequest which Lynn had inherited from her mother. "We had to——"

"But Dad! You mean you have *nothing* left?"

"This house and the car, nothing else. But the money wasn't important. I managed to raise it quietly enough that same day. Ken Sampson, at the bank, is a good friend who wouldn't noise it around. I got it together the way they wanted it, in old bills, mostly twenties. Dick thought we ought to list the numbers, but I wouldn't take even that small chance."

Appalled by the sacrifice imposed on her father, Lynn looked dazedly at the second note. Carrick was pointing to part of the kidnappers' instructions.

"'Wrap money in one package using several thicknesses plastic fabric on outside and seal tight.' That was to make it waterproof. The next morning at four o'clock,

63

following directions exactly, Spence and I went out on the bay in my boat. As the note said we would, we found a praam drifting without a sail—one of the praams used by the junior sailing class at the yacht club. We left the package in it and turned straight back, watching it as long as we could. We saw nothing at all, but we waited, knowing the tide would bring the praam inshore. When it did, the money was gone.''

"A swimmer?" Lynn asked.

"One of the men must have swum from another boat anchored not far away, possibly using a skin-diver's rig, then back. Easy, quiet, and safe. They might as well have been a thousand miles out of reach. They knew that as long as they had you, we wouldn't dare come after them, and of course we didn't.''

"Then that's what they were doing when—— Yesterday morning, while it was still dark, both of them came and stayed longer than usual. They seemed to be busy with something—probably counting and dividing the money." Lynn asked anxiously, "Is there a good chance of getting it back? I don't care about my part of it, but Dad's——"

"We're certainly trying, Lynn," Carrick said, "but we'll need all the help you can give us. About the hide-out, now. Did the men always come and go by water?"

"Sometimes I heard a boat coming, and the motor was shut off at a distance before they came in. Other times I didn't—they were just suddenly there."

Carrick asked his questions expertly. Had she heard any highway traffic nearby? No, she hadn't. A telephone bell ringing? No. A radio playing? Surf? The engine of a private power plant? None of them. Had the men used candles? A lantern? Flashlights? She couldn't tell. Did it have running water? No.

"No bathroom?"

64

"I was never taken to one."

"No outdoor toilet?"

"I don't know." She felt herself turning pale with remembered humiliation. "I'd rather not tell you——"

"Never mind, Lynn." Also embarrassed, Carrick went on. Had either of the men used tobacco—cigarettes, cigar, or pipe? If they had, the strong odour of the air freshener had masked the fragrance of the smoke. Was the place tight or draughty? Tight. Did the door have a lock—had she heard a key used? She hadn't heard, but she thought they kept the door fastened. Twice it had rained while they had her there; had the roof leaked? She thought not. Would she assume the place was unfurnished? She had never been put on a bed or a chair, and the floor was bare. What could she tell them about the floor? It was either hard-packed earth or cement, and there was loose sand on it.

As Carrick turned away Lynn looked down at her left hand. They had not noticed that she wasn't wearing her wedding ring. The explanation of what she had done with it fitted in at this point; but she hesitated.

While giving her answers, Lynn had been puzzled again by Dick Carrick's manner. There was a covert directness in it. He seemed to be aiming his questions at a certain objective. And Dan—he had listened anxiously, as if afraid she might say a wrong thing. Both of them had something in mind that they hadn't told her about. It was strange—Dick reaching for certain information, Dan worried that he would find it. Instinctively she became cautious. She put herself on guard without knowing what she was guarding herself against.

"One more important thing, Lynn."

Carrick had plugged in the tape recorder and made it ready.

"As another precaution they delivered their message in three different ways, from an increasingly safe distance.

It's generally known that a call from a dial phone can't be traced—if it's brief enough it can't be caught even by a technician watching for it inside the exchange. During the night Spence received two calls from one of the snatchers. The first came at about one o'clock, the second almost three hours later. The voice you're about to hear is muffled and disguised, but listen very carefully, Lynn."

He turned the selector switch to *Playback*. For a few seconds the instrument was silent. When the reproduced words came they were low-pitched, slow, and indistinct.

First: "*That's better. Keep them out. Stay alone there. Later tonight.*"

"Then," Carrick said, "at about four o'clock——"

After a silence: "*Peterson's pier. Go to Peterson's pier.*"

Carrick stopped the machine, gazing at Lynn expectantly. "Does it put you in mind of anyone, Lynn? Who does it suggest?"

She shook her head. "Nobody. No one at all."

Carrick frowned with disappointment, and Dan Teague, leaning back in his chair, was obviously relieved.

Spencer Armstead made an impatient noise. "Lynn, there's something about the way it was said, something familiar that——"

Carrick cut in quickly. "Please, Spence. We'll get back to it in a minute. First, let's see how much we've learned." His manner took on a professional briskness. "These two men took great pains to keep you from recognizing them or identifying them later. That's a strong reason for believing one of them is well known to you, Lynn, if not both."

"Not the rough one. I'm sure of that."

"The other, then. Perhaps that accounts for the gentleness you spoke of. Knowing you, even liking you, he didn't want to hurt you."

"But he did, by helping the other. I don't believe I've

ever really hated anyone before. But I do hate them both. For what they did and what they are——" She shivered.

Carrick gave her a long, curious look before going on. "Next, they're still in or near Belle Loma. That's a sound assumption because, for one thing, they were already under cover by the time the search started. I won't go into the other reasons now, but Dan agrees. If this is so, they have the money hidden somewhere nearby and they're waiting for a safe chance to move it out. So far it has been too risky, at least by water. Since sunrise the Coast Guard has been checking all boats on the bay and in the Gulf, under the pretext of making routine examinations, but as of now they've found nothing suspicious. Dan had come to suspect one boat owner, a man named Alec Poole, staying at the Azalea Motel, but it was no good—Poole is in the clear. There are not many other possibilities, Lynn."

"Someone I know?" It disturbed her. "But it's simply not possible, Dick!"

"I'm afraid it's true."

"Is there anyone you suspect?"

An interruption allowed Carrick to avoid the question. Downstairs, a gong sounded.

"Someone at the front door." Unwilling to leave Lynn's side, her father asked, "Tim, would you mind seeing who it is?"

As Hampden left the bedroom Carrick resumed.

"Now, what else do we know? A boat was essential to them. The hide-out is on or near the water. It was a hard, sandy floor, lacks what we call conveniences, and evidently it sits in primitive surroundings. There is a characteristic smell about it, as a place would have if it had been closed up for a long time, or if it's located near a salt flat or marshy land. Lynn, it seems certain they took you to one of the islands in the bay. The only place I can think of, the only one that fits all these conditions, is that old construction-gang shack sitting back in the wilds of Pelican Key."

"But it couldn't possibly be! Griff is over there so much, and Bill's there all the time—it would have been much too dangerous for——" A twinge of alarm stopped her. "Dick, just who do you suspect?"

He answered her carefully. "This will shock you, Lynn. I wish we could duck it, but we can't. I must say none of us came anywhere near suspecting Griff until last night, when he brought it on himself."

Griff? It was too ridiculous; she laughed. But her laughter was suddenly gone. Dick Carrick was actually serious. And her father's face—a fury smouldering in him.

"But what could Griff possibly have done last night to cause you to——"

Spencer Armstead blurted, "He was spying on the place, watching——"

"Please, Spence, let me. Lynn, this is what we saw and heard him doing—an accurate, uncoloured report."

She listened to it—how Griff had twice sneaked past the house, first in his boat and again in his truck, just before midnight; how he had returned and insisted on coming in —and she kept shaking her head incredulously.

"But, Dick, that's just Griff. He often acts on impulse. If he wanted to see me alone—why, once he'd decided, it wouldn't make any difference to him what time it was, he'd simply come."

"But his questions, Lynn!" Spencer Armstead said. "He kept pressing me. He was testing me."

"Testing you?"

Carrick explained. "If Griff had wanted to see whether Spence would break down and let the truth out, he would have asked those same questions in that same persistent way. If he were checking, on the chance that we'd set a trap—if he had come for an inside look at the situation here—— Lynn, he did learn important things—that we had this tape recorder connected to the phone, that Tim and I were here. You remember that first message——"

Carrick flipped the selector switch back and forth and Lynn heard the significant words repeated.

"You see, Lynn? 'Keep them out—stay alone.' The man who said that had to know Tim and I had been here, and Griff did know."

"But anyone watching this place——"

"True," Carrick conceded. "Let's give Griff the benefit of every doubt. Let's believe as long as we can that his coming here in that unusual way was entirely innocent, and that when he went down to the police office next and asked Dan about Hal he was worried that something had happened to you too—because, looking at it fairly, he had reason to think so. But Lynn, that isn't all."

She was still shaking her head—but bracing herself.

"When Griff left this house, I followed him, from the parking lot of the Beachcomber down to the police office, then on to his home. Now understand this, Lynn. At that time I didn't really suspect Griff. I thought his behaviour was puzzling, but hardly suspicious. My reason for checking on him was this. Last night was the most critical time of all—a break in the case was due, one way or the other. I was afraid Griff might do something that would throw a bad scare into the snatchers at the worst time, the last minute. Being anxious about you, but not knowing how great the danger to you was, he could make a wrong move that would be disastrous. If he showed any sign of it, I meant to stop him.

"When he went inside the house I left my car and watched him through a window. He moved around the living-room, worried and restless. I saw him go to the telephone. For no particular reason, just automatically, I noted the time—thirteen minutes past one.

"The call he made was brief. He opened a can of beer and paced around again, drinking it. Then he turned off the lights and went into the bedroom. He was turning in, so I left it at that and went home. Later, after Spence had phoned me and we'd found you on the pier, I listened to that tape recording. Spence had remembered to write down the time when each of the two calls had come in. The first had been at——"

"Exactly one-thirteen," Spencer Armstead said.

Carrick drew a memo pad from his pocket. Lynn recognized her father's forceful handwriting. At the top, the figures 1.13. She stared at it speechlessly.

"Could that be sheer coincidence, Lynn?"

She turned to Dan Teague and saw dismay on his face. She couldn't think; she was fumbling for a possible explanation when the door opened. Tim Hampden stepped in, looking disturbed.

"Griff's downstairs."

Lynn swung up to her feet.

"I tried to get rid of him, but he wouldn't go," Hampden said. "He knows Lynn's here."

Spencer Armstead blurted, "Of course he knows! What more proof do we need? Dan Teague, it's your duty to arrest——"

Carrick said quickly, "No, Spence, not yet!" and at the same time Lynn put her hand on her father's arm. It quieted him. She was gazing downward, and with her other hand she was touching the swollen bruise on her jaw. The four men watched her uncertainly as she moved to the door.

At the head of the stairs she paused, bracing herself against the wall. She heard Griff moving about in the living-room. He was whistling to himself. His long-time favourite, *Ebb Tide*. Now remembrance and recognition struck Lynn together like a double blow.

She was back inside the hide-out at that moment of uncertainty and terror when an alarm had frightened the two men. She could almost feel the rough one's hands again on her throat. She recalled her impression that the second man had gone out to investigate, and how, next, she had heard a man walking about, and Griff's whistling. *Ebb Tide.* It was this same snatch of music, whistled in just this same random way, that she had heard outside the hide-out.

In her half dreams she had thought, no, Griff hadn't been searching for her, because he hadn't checked, hadn't tried to enter. No; she had imagined it. . . . Now she knew she had imagined nothing. It was true—the whistler had actually been Griff.

"One of them is known to you, Lynn. His gentleness—knowing you, even liking you——"

In the living-room below, Griff had paused. Perhaps she had made a sound. Now he was coming towards the base of the stairs. There was a crying in her mind: *I can't, I can't see him now!* She pushed herself away, stumbled back to her bedroom door and pulled it tightly shut behind her.

CHAPTER VII

Alec poole closed the throttle and *Playgirl,* slowing as she passed the flashing red channel-marker, swung into the cove at the northern tip of Pelican Key.

Vina was standing beside him, wearing white short shorts and halter, her one arm across his shoulders, her fingers toying with his hair.

"You certainly came the long way around, Alec. What

was the idea, circling 'way out to nowhere, then coming back? What're we doing here anyway?"

"Taking a boat run, baby."

"I don't believe that. I mean it's more than that. You've got something on your mind, I can tell. It isn't me. You haven't given me any attention at all for days. Alec, what've you been up to?"

"You ask too damn many questions."

"Besides, you told me once this whole island belongs to somebody who's some kind of hermit or something. You said whoever owns it won't let strangers step foot on it, just a few friends. You're not friends with him, are you?"

"Sure, we've been pals since 'way back," Poole said sarcastically. "I drop in on Bill every time I come around here. It's okay with him if I want to fish in the cove or tie up for the night."

"You're lying. You're a terrible liar, Alec. That good-looking young man I saw you talking to here once—was that Bill?"

"No."

"Who was it, then?"

"They call him Griff."

"Griff who?"

"Why don't you pipe down?"

"You won't talk to me. You never tell me anything I want to know. Alec, why did that other boat stop us back there?"

"Coast Guard."

"But why did they stop us and come in and look all around?"

"You heard what the man said. Routine inspection."

"But other times they never looked so much. They were hunting for something special. Alec? Weren't they?"

"How should I know? Anyhow they didn't find anything special, so skip it."

"But why are we being checked up on like this?—like that night and again today. You've been up to something, I know you have, and you won't tell me what it is." She rested her blonde head on his shoulder. "You worry me so."

Impatiently he detached himself from her. She sat in the deck-chair, her sun-tanned legs stretched out, watching him unhappily while he moored the cruiser. The other boat on the opposite side of the pier, ship-shape but old and angular in its lines, must belong to the owner of the island. Vina didn't like this cove. It was too far away from the world. Stoutly sea-walled all around and well sheltered by palms and pines, it was made forbidding by a painted sign almost half as big as a billboard: *POSTED— STAY OUT—No Mooring—No Fishing—STRICTLY PRI- VATE PROPERTY. Wm. Rockwood, Owner.*

The sign didn't mean Alec Poole, though. He certainly wasn't acting like it did.

He put a fish-pole in her hands. "Stay here. Catch a mullet."

"You think I'm ignorant. Mullet are vegetarians. They won't take bait or a lure. If you want mullet you have to use a net or a gaff. You thought I didn't know that, didn't you? Alec, what's that you've got in your pocket?"

"A baby alligator."

"It isn't either. It's something else. I can see that from the way it bulges out, like a can of beer."

"All right, it's a can of beer. Nothing I like better than to go out on the bay with an ice-cold can of beer in my pants pocket and a blonde yakking her dumb head off."

"Alec, where are you going now? Why can't I come with you?"

"For God's sake!" he said in exasperation. "Shut up, stay here and fish. If you see another boat putting in, beep the horn."

73

"Why?"

"Never mind, goddammit! Just do as I say. I'll be a few minutes, that's all."

She obeyed him to the extent of staying there. Dropping the pole to the deck, she watched him moodily as he strode along the pier. He didn't look back at her, but went on at the same rapid pace, following a path towards a cottage of well-weathered cypress. Instead of going to the door, he went farther—around the cottage and out of sight.

She watched the mouth of the cove idly and lonesomely until she heard him coming back. Still in a hurry, he dropped aboard and began casting off the spring lines, snapping at her to help him. She did, eyeing him curiously.

"Was the beer good, Alec?"

"You wanta get smacked?"

"Well, why shouldn't I ask? You haven't got it any more."

"God, there's something I wish you'd learn!—how to get lost."

"You don't really mean that," she said without resentment. "Even if you did, I wouldn't."

The engine started, he sent the *Playgirl* sternwards, then quickly reversed the propeller and veered out of the cove. Once in the open bay he bore into a wide circle, then headed towards the yacht club docks. She saw him peer towards the north and heard him say to himself, "Whew! Pretty close."

Another boat off their starboard bow was heading towards Pelican Key. As it approached, Poole waved a hand fraternally, and as it passed he put on his derisive smile. Its name, Vina saw, was *Julie*. She remembered the handsome, lean-faced man at *Julie*'s wheel; she'd seen him somewhere but didn't know his name. In the cockpit was a girl she had noticed at the yacht club—Lynn Griffith.

74

Vina narrowed her eyes at the third person aboard. He was the one who had banged on her door and poked around her room last night—that snoopy cop.

Dick Carrick, at *Julie*'s wheel, and Lynn, seated behind him, saw the man in the passing boat wave at them in a comradely manner and both waved back. Dan Teague didn't; he simply peered after Alec Poole and the red-headed girl, feeling chagrined because he had been so wrong about them. Once they had cut across *Playgirl*'s wake, all of them forgot her.

Before putting out they had made sure Griff would not be on Pelican Key; *Lotus* was in her home dock. Lynn had persuaded her father to stay at home and rest, and Tim Hampden had gone off to his neglected real estate office. At first she had refused to come, but Carrick had insisted it was necessary—some sort of legal point—and her father had asserted that, in fairness to him, she must "see for herself."

As they entered the cove her eyes lifted to the cypress cottage on the hummock beyond the pier. During the first few weeks of their marriage she had lived there with Griff in complete contentment. Now she was coming back to it unwillingly because her father and Dick Carrick and Tim Hampden—all of them except Dan Teague, she thought—believed that on Pelican Key they might find more evidence to prove her husband was an abhorrent criminal.

After Carrick had moored *Julie* and Dan Teague had helped Lynn up to the pier, they went together to the foot of the path that curved through patches of palmetto towards the cottage. Carrick paused there, giving her an inquiring look, and she saw Teague's expression of sorry uncertainty.

"Something's not right about it, Dick," Lynn insisted. "When they took me out they did seem to carry me along

75

a path that winds just like this one. Then why was it straight and short when they took me in?"

"You were only half conscious then, Lynn," Carrick reminded her.

"But I remember the rest clearly enough—I've told you how they put me down on the ground before they went in to use the spray. And it was level ground, not sloping like this."

"Shocked and confused as you were, Lynn——" Carrick said. "And naturally you're inclined to give Griff the benefit of every doubt."

Following Griff's visit to her father's home—after he had left without seeing her—Lynn had faced his guilt as a staggering fact. The telephone call at 1.13 and Griff's undeniable presence outside the hide-out had combined to make it a dreadful certainty. She had recoiled from it wholly, but she had been too stunned then to see any possible escape from it. Soon she had found herself hammering at it with a hard loyalty, a conviction that Griff was incapable of inflicting such cruelty—such *planned* cruelty— on her, or on anyone at all. When she tried to think how to explain away those damning circumstances it seemed hopeless. Yet she could not stop believing an explanation could be found; and no one should be better able or could be more eager to find it than she, the victim.

"So let her," Dan Teague was saying curtly to Carrick. "Let her give Griff the benefit of the doubt. Somebody should. You've put me where I never expected to be, on the fence. But Lynn—— When and if *she* winds up convinced, that'll make a case."

"I'm telling the truth," Lynn said. "I have to, for Dad's sake and Griff's too. But I know I'm not mistaken about that first night. I honestly believe I wasn't brought here. Coming in, they simply couldn't have carried me a straight, short distance to any place on Pelican Key."

76

Carrick did not comment again. They followed the path, Lynn leading the way, until they reached the cottage door.

"I don't want to do this." She had paused there. "It's sneaking behind Griff's back."

"Sneaking behind a criminal's back, as you put it, is one way to catch him," Carrick remarked. "On the other hand, if we find no evidence at all around here, it will be a strong point in Griff's favour."

The door was unlocked. Lynn went in slowly, feeling her way. A warm sense of belonging returned to her; yet she was an intruder leading unfriendly forces.

She stood still, gazing all around the living-room, paying no attention as Carrick and Teague began their search. This cottage and Griff were inseparables. Griff's father had built it, mostly with his own hands, following the collapse of the historic land boom of the twenties. Belle Loma had been a tiny fishing village then, accessible only by ferry. Every board and beam, every nail had been loaded aboard boats at Palmport, freighted across the bay, unloaded, and laboriously lugged to this secluded spot; and five-year-old Griff had helped his father as best he could to combine these rough parts into a home of rare charm and individuality. Lynn understood, because she had absorbed the understanding from Griff, that this was not merely a house—it was a symbol, a small figment of a grand dream that had never materialized.

She stood in the doorway of the room which Griff had used as his office and which formerly had been his father's studio. Frank Griffith had been a prominent and talented architect. The walls here were covered with his drawings and maps—time-faded now; they were more than thirty years old. They pictured the dream—Bill Rockwood and Griff's father, in partnership, had planned to transform this island jungle into a lotus land, to create on Pelican

77

Key a sanctuary of beautiful homes for tranquil tropical living.

The cove was to have become a fine yacht basin; there were to have been swimming-pools, tennis-courts, a golf-course, a skeet field, even an air-strip and a small luxury hotel. Work had scarcely begun when the great land bubble burst. Frank Griffith's age-dimmed plans and drawings in this room, and the duplicates in Bill Rockwood's house, were all that remained of the dream. Today Pelican Key was still the wilderness it had been then, unchanged—except in Griff's eyes. Having lived since childhood with his father's vision, he had made it his own—and just as vainly, because it was too big for him and he could not summon the necessary resources to bring it into being.

Turning away, Lynn found Carrick coming from the kitchen and Teague from the bedroom. They were empty-handed. This search had been perfunctory; they hadn't actually expected to find any evidence in the cottage. The urgency in Carrick's movements suggested that their next move would be more important. Lynn knew they meant to go now to the old construction-gang shack far back on the island, and misgivings stirred in her.

The cottage behind them, they followed another narrow path flanked by thickets of palmetto. To their left, on a low, sandy hillock above the beach, Bill Rockwood's home was visible past stands of shaggy palms. Bill was there, Lynn knew, but if he saw them he evidently didn't intend to show himself. It passed from sight as they went on, and suddenly the path broadened before them.

This was a street, or what had been planned as a street before the golden project was abandoned. It had been cleared by bulldozers and tamped rock-hard but left un-paved. Thinly carpeted by trailing honeysuckle now, it led nowhere. There were kerbstones on both sides and,

78

almost concealed by tall weeds, cement sidewalks vanishing into the jungle.

The shack, built of pine sheathing, roofed with asphalt shingles, and windowless, was almost closed in by masses of hibiscus bushes and mulberry trees. The path did not lead to the door but around to a trash pile in the rear. Farther behind it the ground was marshy beneath a tangle of mangroves. As they left the path Dick Carrick paused to look at Lynn inquiringly again, reminding her of the mal-odour of rotting vegetation thickening the air.

"But this isn't the place, Dick. It couldn't be. For one thing, it's too far from the water."

Carrick pointed to a green-scummed inlet between the swamp and the shore. It was narrow and shallow, but through it a small boat might be brought in fairly close at high tide.

Teague put in a demurrer. "I don't see any footprints in that soft ground around there."

"And don't forget I heard a man walking on gravel or crushed sea-shell," Lynn said. "There isn't any here."

In answer, Carrick indicated the matting of dry palm fronds that had fallen all around. He stepped on one of them. It gave off a faint rustling and crackling.

"Possible?" he asked.

She shook her head in confusion. "I don't know, I was so frightened. But there *is* a way I can tell for certain whether or not they kept me in this place."

Carrick lifted his eyebrows at her. "This is something you hadn't mentioned before, Lynn. How can you do that?"

"Dick, it's true. When we find the place they used as their hide-out, I'll be perfectly sure of it. It's something those two men don't know about, I'm almost positive they don't—no one else in the world knows it, only me, and I want to keep it to myself."

"But why that?"

"Because it's something that can't be changed or twisted to point to Griff if he isn't guilty. But if he is—if the hide-out *is* connected with Griff, then it will be enough to convince even me."

Carrick looked dubious. "This proof of yours, Lynn—— If you do find it, you won't keep it from us any longer?"

She felt her cheeks stiffen. "I won't hold out, Dick. I couldn't. If it shows Griff is guilty, I'll want terribly not to tell you—but I will."

Teague and Carrick were frowning at her. The dread in her eyes persuaded the chief. Carrick still disapproved, but the pain of Lynn's sincerity and resolution left him no room for argument.

"All right, Lynn," Carrick said. "We'll do this your way."

"I—I'm going in alone."

They stood back as she went to the door and put her hand on the knob. She began bringing vividly back to mind every detail she could remember about the hide-out and checking them against the moment's reality.

The knob turned with a slight squeak. As she pushed the door open the hinges gave off a rusty noise. Could she have heard these through the ear-plugs? She didn't know. The moment she stepped inside a strong smell struck her— the mustiness of long disuse combined with the trapped fetor of the swamp. She tried to find a lingering trace of the deodorizer and could not. . . . So far it was neither yes nor no.

Had she heard any highway traffic nearby? A telephone ringing, a radio playing, surf? No, none of them. Other than the crunching of gravel underfoot—or dry palm fronds—she had discerned only a lapping of water and motor-boats passing at vague distances; and she could hear both these sounds now.

Was the place tight or draughty; *Tight*—and this crude shack, meant only as a temporary shelter for tools and small equipment, had no windows.

Unfurnished? There was nothing inside it except a rusted marine engine, a fuel drum, random lengths of lumber, and a pile of weathered rope.

The floor? Like this one—hard-packed earth covered with a thin scattering of tracked-in sand. It was the floor that would tell Lynn the final answer.

She had thought of it during the second night, an idea born of her loathing for the man who had struck her with his fist. Alone there, lying with one shoulder against the wall, she had worked her wedding-ring off her finger. She had pressed the ring against the floor at the base of the wall and had brushed a little sand over it to hide it. Unless by some freak of bad luck the two men had found it after taking her away, it must be there still.

When Lynn closed the door behind her the inside of the shack was darkened only a little; light shone in through the spaces under the eaves. She began in the nearest corner, using her flattened hand to clear away the loose grit at the edge of the floor. Her fingers felt cold as she worked along; she found herself trembling. Her wedding-ring, if she found it here, would inevitably brand with guilt the man who had pledged his love to her when placing it on her finger.

When she straightened finally she leaned against the wall, drawing in a shivering breath. She had not found it. She had been thorough, inch by inch, and she was certain the ring was not here.

She was smiling when she stepped outside. "Dick, this is not the place. This is *not* the place."

Blinking in the sudden bright sunlight, she saw that they had moved back and were standing on the path. Both of them were looking at her with a strange soberness.

"Lynn—— Here, please," and Carrick beckoned. She went with them and they led her to the rear of the shack. The trash pile was an accumulation of years of rusted cans and other debris.

"We haven't touched this so far," Carrick said. "First we wanted you to see it for yourself, just as we spotted it."

He covered his hand with his handkerchief and reached down to a bright new can. The printing on the metal read, in part, *Atmosweet Air Freshener*. Carrick shook it and said, "Almost empty." He pressed the valve and a plume of vapour spewed out.

Lynn recoiled instantly, her hand pressed over her face. Carrick and Teague did not need to ask her whether this was the same scent the snatchers had used. Her revulsion, the startled disbelief in her eyes were answer enough.

"How do you account for this, Lynn?" Carrick asked quietly.

"I can't! But there's something wrong, Dick. It doesn't belong here. This isn't the place, it isn't!"

Neither Carrick nor Teague answered. The chief's face was pale with shocked anger, Carrick's set and cold.

"Somebody else could have put that can here," Lynn insisted, "—planted it. Someone who's trying to frame Griff——"

"Lynn, stop and think," Carrick broke in. "Do you believe the snatchers have meant from the beginning to point suspicion towards Griff? Has there been any other sign of it?"

"No, but——"

"No other sign at all," Carrick agreed. "It was Griff's own actions that put the seed in our minds. Is that a fair proposition, Lynn—to say that until now, at least, there has not been a single sign of anyone's intention to frame Griff?"

Her answer came hard—unwilling but fair. "Yes."

82

"All right. Remember that until you told us a deodorizer had been used nobody was aware of it except you yourself and the two snatchers. To the rest of us it came as a surprise. After you'd mentioned it, how many more knew? Four of us—your father, Tim, Dan, and me, and that's all. Nobody except you and we four knows that Griff is even open to suspicion. Now, Lynn—*if* this can *was* planted here, which of us do you think did it? Which of us *could* have done it?"

Lynn could not answer.

"Aside from a total lack of motive, Lynn," Carrick went on quietly, "there's the element of time. Your father and Tim stayed back in Belle Loma. You've been with Dan and me all along—we came with you from your house to mine, then directly here. We're all ruled out."

"I didn't mean any of you——"

"What's more, you didn't tell us the brand name of the spray, because you couldn't, you didn't know; yet this is the same kind the snatchers used." Carrick was shaking his head. "Don't you see now how impossible it is?—unless you suspect that one of the four of us has an accomplice. Do you actually——?"

"Of course not!" Lynn blurted.

"I'm sure you didn't," Carrick said. "One other thing. If this can was really a plant, it must have been put here by someone who had somehow learned we suspect Griff, who decided quickly to use it against him, and rushed over for that purpose only a very short time ago, perhaps only a few minutes before we put in. We did see a boat, and only one, heading from this general direction——"

"Alec Poole's," Dan Teague cut in acridly. "And Poole's in the clear."

"So there you have it," Carrick said. "A frame-up? No, definitely not."

Lynn watched, wordlessly bewildered, as Carrick formed

the handkerchief loosely around the can and held it by its corners so as to avoid effacing latent fingerprints. It must be handled carefully, his manner said, and kept safe as important leading evidence against Griff.

But there *was* something wrong about all this, her stunned mind insisted. Because this wasn't the place, she *knew* it wasn't. Something was dreadfully wrong—but she could not think what it was or how to begin to put it right.

CHAPTER VIII

Never, dan teague told himself sourly, never before had he disliked his job, but he disliked it heartily now.

They were in Dick Carrick's car, with Carrick driving and Lynn seated between them, heading down Gulf Boulevard in Belle Loma. Since returning from Pelican Key they had had little to say to one another. Carrick seemed satisfied to let the evidence speak for itself, and Teague was damned glad of that. He was too queasy in his stomach to want to talk about it, but he couldn't get it out of his mind; and the more he kept hashing it over the more it sickened him. The fact was, this thing about Griff was losing him some of his professional tough-mindedness.

The sun setting in the Gulf was a blazing splendour for which none of them had a glance. Instead, Teague looked at Lynn, so self-absorbed in her frightened bewilderment, and felt a deep and hopeless sort of sympathy for her. Her own sense of fairness and her loyalty to her father were forcing her to help build a capital charge against her husband —a very rough thing. Teague wanted powerfully to get her out of the middle, but how could he? Personally, as Griff's friend, he could think, "To hell with the evidence,

I know the guy too well to believe it," but as a responsible officer he couldn't possibly ignore it. He was letting Carrick take the lead because he would like nothing better than to see the case fall apart in Carrick's own hands; but instead, every step was taking them in deeper and making it worse. And now they were about to take another.

Carrick eased the car to a stop under a clump of pines on Sixth Street. The Gulf lay behind them now. In the distance a hazy lavender dusk lay over Palmport. Lights were sparkling in the marinas and glowing in the windows along the waterfront. Griff's house sat directly ahead.

"He's there," Lynn said.

"I'll check," Teague suggested.

Walking slowly across Belle Loma Way, Teague found himself thinking that there was one important question which nobody had voiced so far: If Griff actually was one of the two snatchers, who was the other? Griff had plenty of friends, including a few backwash bums, and a fifty-fifty split of two hundred thousand dollars could be an overpowering temptation to almost anybody. Aside from that question, the thing that puzzled Teague the most was why all the evidence that had turned up pointed to Griff and none of it to the accomplice.

Teague went in the gate of the basket-weave fence that bordered Griff's neat Zoysia lawn. He could still argue with himself in Griff's defence. For example, Carrick had stressed the point that this pair of snatchers were two very sharp operators. They had thought of everything; they had taken meticulous pains to block every conceivable lead; yet, suddenly, a glaring piece of carelessness had come to light—that almost-empty deodorizer can on the trash pile. The inconsistency of it bothered Teague. There were only two ways about it—either it was valid evidence or it wasn't. If not, the assumption raised new questions. First, the snatchers had got away fast and clean, without

85

leaving a single workable clue, so why would they bother to frame anyone at all? And second, having decided on a frame-up for some secondary purpose of their own, why had they picked Griff as their scapegoat?

Teague could think of a good, solid possibility: if Griff were convicted—not necessarily in court, but in Lynn's mind—a reconciliation between them would become unthinkable and a divorce inevitable.

Pausing at the door, Teague realized there were no longer any lights in the windows. He knocked anyhow. An answer came, not from inside, but from the pier—Griff calling. Teague circled the house and found Griff aboard *Lotus*, about to cast off. Griff waited, holding a line bighted around a piling. Teague pushed his cap back on his head, frowning down at him.

"You look sort of sore at the world, kid," the chief remarked.

"I'm sore all right," Griff answered. "Frustrated. I keep running up against a blank wall and I can't find out what's behind it. You—you're part of it."

"Just call me Stonewall Teague."

"It's true. You were at Lynn's father's place this afternoon. Driving past, I saw your car there. What's up? Why aren't you letting me in on it?"

"After all, Spencer Armstead is our senior commissioner. I drop over there pretty often on town business."

"Damn it, Dan, all I want is a chance to talk things over with Lynn, but something's getting in between us, keeping me from seeing her. Why can't I get a straight story? Last night her father told me she'd be away for several more days, but she got back this morning."

Teague kept his voice as casual as possible. "How'd you find that out, Griff?"

"Happened to run into Doc Elder this afternoon. He told me."

86

Teague let out a long breath. So simply and quickly one suspicious circumstance was explained away! He was relieved to be rid of it, even though other, darker circumstances remained, seemingly inexplicable except in terms of Griff's guilt.

"Doc Elder said she'd been in an auto accident," Griff added. "Banged up a little, not serious—but that's no reason why I shouldn't see her. In fact, it's a good reason why I should."

The "auto accident" was the excuse they had agreed on to account for Lynn's bruised jaw. Teague shrugged and commented, "Well, you know how her father fusses over her, any little thing. Try again later."

"I intend to." Griff was eyeing him. "Did you drop over here with something special on your mind?"

"Nothing better to do." It was clear to Teague that Griff meant to spend the night on Pelican Key. "Sweet dreams, kid."

"Yeah," Griff said dispiritedly. "Same to you."

Teague stood on the pier watching until *Lotus* was well under way, then turned and walked back to the gate. His mouth twisting in distaste, he waved an arm, signalling to Carrick and Lynn in the waiting car. *All clear*, it meant. *You can come on and search the house now.*

What was that line he had quoted to Griff last night? "A policeman's lot is not a happy one." He hadn't known by half how truly he had spoken.

Steering *Lotus* automatically on the long-familiar course, Griff began glancing about the deck. To a sporting yachtsman this boat might have seemed disgracefully untidy and neglected. But it was not a spit-and-polish pleasure craft; actually it was as shipshape as Griff could keep it. Broad-beamed and sturdy, a kind of amphibious truck essential to Griff in his work, it bore the occupational scars

87

of a veteran labourer. In Griff's eyes it was in good order; but he sensed something not quite right about it tonight, or something alien, as if strangers had been aboard in his absence.

He tried to dismiss the feeling but it wouldn't leave him. There was a strong rapport between *Lotus* and her owner; she seemed to be trying to communicate a message. Part of his mind puzzled over it as he ran on, but he was too preoccupied, too obscurely troubled about Lynn to pay it much attention.

He heard a *halloo-o*, pulled his thoughts back aboard and looked around. Unconsciously he had followed the channel to a point within a mile or so of the cove of Pelican Key. He cut his engine to idling. On his port bow another vessel was veering towards him under low power—a familiar patrol boat flying both the Coast Guard ensign and, above it, the commission pennant, indicating it was on duty. Several men aboard were watching Griff with friendly grins. Among them Griff saw Bob Sage, the commander of the station on Belmore Key.

"Tub ahoy!" Sage called. "Where you taking that thing?"

"Where do you think, you joker?" Griff's smile grew as the patrol boat drew abeam. "You boys have been cutting capers around this bay all day long. Even the big brass is working for a change. How come?"

"General safety check-off, that's all," the commander answered. "Making it rough for some of these hot-rod skippers. We won't waste any time on you, though. Wouldn't risk coming aboard that bucket of yours anyhow."

Griff said, "Ha!" He had been a volunteer member of the Coast Guard Auxiliary for more than ten years; they knew without checking that he carried more than the legally required equipment.

"Say, Griff——" Sage raised his voice as the two boats pulled apart. "If you see anything unusual—let us know?"

"What's that mean?"

Sage's answer was lost in the roar of the patrol boat's exhaust as it put on increased power. Griff stared after it. For the life of him he couldn't figure all this out—Dan Teague waiting for an emergency to break last night, the helicopter beating around before dawn, the rash of boat inspections today with the commander himself in charge—and everybody being so damned close-mouthed. The worst of it was an exasperatingly intangible connection with Lynn and Griff's inability to reach her.

Tomorrow he *would* see her and get to the bottom of this business. First thing tomorrow morning, he promised himself, he would go back to Spencer Armstead's house and demand——

Sharply he lifted his head. *Lotus*'s message had broken through—a warning of danger. He had caught a strong whiff of raw gasoline.

Quickly he switched off the motor. While *Lotus* slowed, steering herself, he began a quick check-up. He was too experienced a boatman to ignore for a single moment the risk of a fire or an explosion at sea. A few ounces of fuel, vaporized and mixed with air, packed the destructive power of a dozen sticks of dynamite, and any small spark might set it off.

He opened the hatch of the engine compartment, and an invisible cloud of vapour surged up. Startled, he stepped back and reached to the switch of the bilge blower. Most electrical contacts were to be strictly avoided now, but this was safe enough; the electric fans in the ventilator ducts below were tightly enclosed in fine-mesh screen—but to judge from the concentration of the fumes, the bilges would be a long time clearing.

It bewildered Griff. He never neglected his fuel system;

he made a point of inspecting it periodically and took care to keep every coupling tight; yet there was a bad leak somewhere below, transforming the *Lotus* into a powder-keg.

Darkness was settling rapidly now; Griff could see little in the engine compartment. He knelt and reached down to the copper fuel line. It should be bone dry, but it was wet, almost dripping. He slid his hand along quickly, first closed the shut-off valve at the tank, then the other at the carburettor. The tubing seemed to be bent. And another thing—— Although he couldn't be entirely certain in this dim light, it appeared that the storage battery was missing its safety cover—its terminals were exposed—and that, too, was as unaccountable as it was dangerous.

Griff couldn't believe this damage had been intentionally done—there was no reason on earth why anyone should want to sabotage his boat—but someone *had* been below. Who? Doing what?

He straightened, turned away, and worked the bilge-pump. It discharged a turgid, pulsing stream that put an iridescence on the dark surface of the bay—oil, but mostly gasoline. There was an appalling amount of liquid fuel washing about on the surface of the bilge water, and as the blowers exhausted the vapour below the deck, more vapour was forming. It meant that the gasoline line had been leaking for some time, Griff couldn't guess how many hours. Until this hazard was eliminated he wouldn't dare start the motor again. He couldn't go below to locate and repair the damage until the air in the engine compartment became breathable.

Lotus wallowed gently and heavily, adrift in the deepening twilight. The blowers hummed steadily while Griff waited and worried. Fuel leaks like this one, he knew, had killed many a careless boatman. The all-important thing was to avoid creating a spark, however small.

Finally, judging that he had waited long enough, Griff

turned to his tool-box, selected an adjustable wrench, and lowered himself into the engine compartment. To use a flashlight would be too dangerous; he would have to work without one, by feel. He squeezed himself down beside the engine, found the tank fitting and tightened it. His hand followed the fuel line to the carburettor, and again he used the wrench. Neither connection seemed to have been at fault. Perhaps, Griff thought, the vibration of the motor, or the bending of the fuel line, had opened a tiny crack in the tubing itself.

Griff paused, listening. Had he heard another boat nearby? Evidently not—there was no sound now.

Immediately he went back to work. He had no time to waste. The darkness was thickening rapidly and the gas fumes were beginning to make him dizzy.

He twisted himself about, trying to see, and as he did so he noticed something odd, something he had never seen before. It was dull-white and square, some kind of bundle wedged in between the deck beams.

With his fingers he explored it, frowning in bewilderment. He found that nails had been driven into the beams and that a wire, twisted around them, was holding the package against the underside of the deck.

He worked at the wire, loosened it, and pulled the package free. Straightening in the hatch, and drawing a deep breath to clear his head, he frowned over it. A package tightly and smoothly wrapped. Griff reached up, placed it on the deck beside the hatch, then ducked down again to search further.

Although he could see almost nothing in the compartment now, there seemed to be a second package wired in place between the deck beams farther forward. As he stretched his hand towards it, hampered in his movements, he felt his left shoulder pressing against the fuel line. Immediately he drew back, realizing that this was the answer,

91

the cause of the leak. The line had been bent inadvertently by a man crowding himself into this cramped space, a man working quickly with hammer and wire to hide the two packages beneath the deck.

Dizzy again, Griff drew back, leaving the second package in place. As his head came above the deck he saw a movement. The first package was not where he had left it. It was being lifted; Griff saw a hand on it, a hand swinging, then the package thrown. It went sailing through the darkness, far overboard.

Next, too bewildered to understand what was happening, Griff looked up at something that was towering above him—a man, all black against the sky, one arm swiping down at him.

Griff tried to duck the blow. As he toppled aside a terrifying thought streaked through his confusion. The wrench! He had been holding the wrench in his left hand and he had dropped it.

He heard it hit metal. The storage battery! The wrench had struck across the exposed terminals. Instantly a powerful, spluttering spark shot through the darkness below.

Griff was conscious of the explosion only as a blast of forces lifting him and propelling him out of the compartment like a cork popped out of a bottle.

The chill of the water shocked him back to stunned awareness. He was choking. He clawed and his head came above the surface. Instinctively he kept himself afloat. His vision was blurred, his ears full of a dull ringing, but he was vaguely aware of debris in the water around him—broken boards, spears of wood jabbing him with their sharp points.

He heard the thrumming of a motor-boat and twisted himself about, blearily looking for it. He could not find *Lotus*—except for a dark mass of wreckage she was gone.

There were no running lights visible anywhere nearby. Griff shook his head, trying to clear his senses. Still there were no lights, but the sound continued—the churning of an unseen boat.

Griff called—a hoarse, strangling sound—then listened. Had his voice carried? Was the boat coming to help him? No, it was heading away. . . . *Away?* He yelled again. He couldn't believe it, but the lightless boat was heading away at top speed.

A consuming weakness took hold of Griff. The blurred lights of Belle Loma seemed far off—unreachably far. He wrenched himself about, towards Pelican Key, and tried to swim. His arms were lead. He lifted them laboriously, dropped them, forgot them. He felt his head drooping below the surface and then the world was gone.

The explosion was heard all along the bay front. It occurred some ten minutes after Carrick and Lynn had left Dan Teague at the town offices. Staring out of the door, mulling over the fact that their search of Griff's house had been fruitless, he saw the angry red flash far out over the bay. By the time the sound boomed in he was running across Belle Loma Way towards the ramp where the fire department's motor surf-boat was tied up.

The big bang released a flurry of activity in Belle Loma. By the time Teague had the patrol boat in the water, the outboard started, one patrolman and two volunteer firemen had joined him. Putting out, they heard other boats getting under way from private piers nearby.

Towards the south a searchlight sprang out of the night, a brilliant beam sweeping the water. That would be the Coast Guard patrol boat, Teague knew. He judged that the explosion had occurred not far from the northern tip of Pelican Key. Nearing the spot, he found the water thick with floating litter and small boats converging upon it.

93

The searchlight of the patrol boat steadied, pin-pointing something in the water. Teague swung towards it. The Coast Guard boat slowed and a man dropped overboard. Teague watched as the trained swimmer expertly performed his rescue work. A limp man was hauled up, water streaming from his clothes. It was Griff. Close alongside now, Teague saw Griff trying to ward off his rescuers and struggling to stay on his feet.

"Griff, were you alone?" This was Bob Sage, gripping Griff's arms to hold him still. "Griff, can you understand me? Was anybody else aboard?"

Griff sputtered. "Yes—somebody——"

"Somebody else? Who was it?"

"What? What say?"

"Griff, listen. Did you take somebody out in your boat?"

"No, nobody. Put out alone——"

"Which is it, Griff? First you said yes, now you say no. Was anybody else——?"

The questioning ended there. Griff toppled into the arms of the men gathered around him, and they lowered him to the deck.

"Can't tell—but he's going ashore fast!"

"Bob!" Dan Teague called. "Is he badly hurt?"

The patrol boat swung away. Its searchlight swept over several of the smaller boats that were skirting about. One of them held Teague's attention—an antiquated cruiser with an awkward high, boxlike cabin. It was Bill Rockwood's *Carry On*. Rockwood, a paunchy, bald, solemn-faced man, was allowing *Carry On* to drift while he leaned over the transom, scanning the choppy water.

The searchlight blinked out as the patrol boat gained speed, heading towards the municipal pier at Belle Loma. Teague and the men with him used their electric lanterns, circling.

"Something here," Teague said, and reached to a floating object. He pulled it aboard, staring at it—a square white package—but he had no time to examine it closely. Behind him a voice blurted, "Look! What's that? Over there. Another man!"

The man was floating face down, motionless. The chief reached again, grabbed the wet shirt collar, and pulled him up. A coldness seized Teague. The man's skull was grotesquely crushed, the whole top of it smashed in. As Teague stared, a pinkish colour, dead blood mixed with primeval sea-water, spread downwards over the face of Alec Poole.

CHAPTER IX

THROUGH THE WINDOW Lynn saw two cars turning into the driveway, one directly behind the other. The first was the police sedan, the second Tim Hampden's familiar, years-old coupé. Dan Teague alighted with a square white package in his hands. Hampden hurried forward, stared at it, and nodded, identifying it. They turned to the house then, and Lynn hurried to the front door. As they entered she was dismayed by the stiffness of Hampden's face and the deep indignation in Teague's eyes.

She had been waiting restlessly since the chief had phoned, more than an hour ago, to tell her father what had occurred on the bay. Her impulse had been to go straight away to Griff. He was hurt; she belonged with him; but her father had forbidden it obdurately. "There's nothing you can do for him," Dick Carrick had pointed out, and in order to avoid "complicating a ticklish situation", as he had put it to her, she had forced herself to wait. But now her first quick question was for Griff.

"How is he now, Dan?"

The chief gave her a troubled look, went on to the desk, and placed the package there. Spencer Armstead stood glowering at it as Carrick began stripping off the seals of adhesive tape—undoubtedly tape from the same roll that the kidnappers had used on Lynn herself. Teague was relieved to have the offensive thing off his hands. He turned away and, finding Lynn's eyes still questioning him, he answered.

"It's a miracle he wasn't killed. He's suffering from shock, too confused to talk sense so far, and his face and hands are flash-burned, but not badly. He's not even going to the hospital. Doc Elder's taking care of him, and he'll be okay right there in the first-aid room, at least until morning."

"He's tough, you know," Lynn said, "on the outside."

"As tough as the spot he's in."

"Dan—— I don't understand what happened."

"I don't either. But I know this much. If it was anybody else but Griff—— He'd better have a damned good explanation, that's all. The way it looks now—— Open and shut."

The note of disaffection in his voice hurt Lynn. Her own faith in Griff had been badly shaken again. She had looked to Teague for support, but she realized now she had hoped for too much. Teague's esteem for Griff was being torn out of him bit by bit. Circumstances were forcing the chief's office to take full command of the man. It left her with a harsh sense of abandonment.

"You're angry, Dan. At Griff?"

"At myself mostly. As a cop I've been one great big damn boob."

They both turned at the sound of ripping paper. Carrick was opening the inner wrapping of the package, exposing bundles of bank notes. Tim Hampden stood watching gravely while Carrick and Lynn's father made a quick count.

The room was quiet until Carrick said, looking up, "Half. Exactly half. So there must be another bundle like this one."

"I sent the patrol boat out to look again, but——" Teague shook his head. "Whatever became of the other one, your guess is as good as mine." Lynn saw him scowling at himself. "Or better."

Spencer Armstead said flatly, "Griff was in possession of this ransom money. He had it in his boat There's no question about that."

Lynn stared at her father. One hundred thousand dollars had been recovered and returned to him, yet he had shown no sign of gratitude or relief. To him it was money secondarily; chiefly it was another piece of evidence condemning Griff.

Carrick was frowning at Teague. "This bundle wouldn't be easy to hide on any small boat. Griff had it aboard, yet the Coast Guard didn't spot it. Why not? Who bungled?"

"Why not ask Bob Sage about that? He was under your orders, not mine. I'll shoulder my own blame, but——" Disgustedly the chief broke off and explained. "Hell, they didn't even search Griff's boat. A boat that's moored is usually not subject to inspection anyway, and Griff's had been tied up for a couple of days. Besides, they know him so well—he's one of them, the last guy they'd ever question. So naturally they skipped him."

"Naturally!" Spencer Armstead said with sharp scorn. "He counted on that. He knew he could sneak the money out right past them. That's obvious."

Lynn sat silent, hurt by her father's unyielding animosity.

"Was tonight," Carrick asked, "the first time Griff had used his boat since the money was passed?"

Teague's mouth was a sour twist. "Yes."

"Then no further evidence is needed," Spencer Armstead stated impatiently. "This is final proof."

"Not so fast, Spence," Carrick said. "Moral certainty is not enough. An incident of this kind can be extremely tricky under the rules of evidence. Let's take it a little more carefully, step by step."

Lynn thought that Dick Carrick, unlike her father, held no personal prejudice against Griff; yet he was plainly convinced of Griff's guilt. Tim Hampden, quiet and withdrawn, thinking fixedly of the brutal assault on Hal, could not put down his bitterness. Trying to understand them, Lynn told herself that her father was a righteous and aggrieved man. Dan was Griff's friend, Dick and Tim were hers. None of them was malicious. They were not persecutors. *Can it be possible all of them are wrong—possible that all four are completely and dreadfully wrong?* In a torment of uncertainty, listening to them convicting her husband, Lynn could do no more than hope to hear something, some little thing, that might be of help to Griff.

"Dan," Carrick said, "you saw Griff putting out in his boat tonight."

Lynn listened intently as Teague answered, "Alone. I'm sure of that. When he shoved off nobody else was aboard that boat."

"Then what about this man Alec Poole?" Carrick asked with a bite in his voice. "This man you thought was entirely in the clear."

Teague's face coloured with self-reproach and embarrassment. "All right, I admit it, I made a mistake. Poole played me for a fool. Looking back, I can see through the trick he pulled, now that it's too late—now that he's dead and can't talk—but I didn't then."

"What else got past you, Dan?" Carrick asked pointedly. "Had you ever seen Poole and Griff together?"

"Not that I remember."

"But they were accomplices, Dan, obviously."

"They were damn careful not to let it show. There was nothing suspicious between them. Except——"

"Except what?"

"Tonight, after the explosion, Frank Anson"—the chief had named one of his patrolmen—"said he'd noticed Poole hanging around Griff's end of town off and on during the day."

"Keeping an eye on Griff's boat because the ransom money was hidden in it," Carrick said. "Wasn't he questioned?"

"The man was fishing off the sea wall, that's all. Why the hell should he be—— No! No, he wasn't questioned because we didn't have the advantage you have now—a pretty keen hindsight." Teague glared. "I'm simply reporting facts," and he clamped his jaw.

Carrick pressed his questions. "Has Poole a criminal record?"

"Never had a reason to pull a file on him."

Tim Hampden spoke up. "I can tell you something about Poole. He was in real estate in Sarasota a few years ago, and he just missed getting jailed for a petty racket he was working. He used forged leases. That is, he'd lease a place for a certain price, then turn a forged copy in to his office, one showing a lower rental figure, and pocket the difference. He was lucky to squeeze out of that one. Later he had the gall to ask me for an agent's job here. He couldn't get honest work anywhere. He was the type for this, all right—he'd go for any kind of dough, crooked or not, little or big, including a kidnapping." There was cold hatred in Hampden's face. "Poole must have been the one who did that to Hal—beat him and kicked him and ran the car over him."

Carrick was eyeing Teague. "You didn't know Poole's background, Dan?"

"I'd heard some talk. That's why I checked on him first thing after Lynn was back home. But I still say there was no good reason at that time——"

"There's good reason now. Poole was aboard Griff's boat when it blew up. Wasn't he, Dan? Is or is that not a fact?"

Lynn was frightened by the heated resentment in Teague's face. His grip on himself was insecure; but he kept it. "Poole must have been standing on the cockpit deck near the engine compartment. He took the force of it in his legs. Broken, both of them. As for the condition of Poole's head, smashed in as it was—— The doc and Judge Tyne"—the acting coroner of Palmport County—"were in a huddle when I left, about how——"

"Let's leave that point until later, Dan, and stick to this one. It's a certainty that Poole was in Griff's boat tonight with one of the two bundles of ransom money, if not both. The question is, why? Where and when did he come aboard?"

"I wasn't there," Teague said stiffly. "All I know is what Griff said when he was pulled out of the bay. He claimed he'd put out alone, but at the same time he admitted somebody was aboard when the boat blew up." Teague went on sticking to his facts with an effort. "Trying to figure that out, I stopped at the Azalea Motel on my way here. Poole's boat was docked in its usual place. The——"

"That girl of Poole's, what's her name?"

"Vina Daly."

"Did you see her?"

"She drove in while I was there. She'd been in Palmport shopping and didn't know what had happened. Before I could get at her one of the other guests at the motel popped off with the news that Poole was dead. She screamed and sobbed, went into hysterics—couldn't hear any questions, much less answer. I'll go back later for another try. I also——"

The telephone interrupted. Answering the call, Spencer Armstead turned a look of long suffering on Dick Carrick. Knowing it was Julia again, Carrick tried to keep a look of annoyance off his face and didn't quite succeed.

"Dick, dinner's just ruined," Julia began. "You said you'd be home for dinner an hour ago and I had it all ready for you. Now it's spoiled, because there you are at the Armstead place again. Again! I might have known."

"I'm sorry, Julie, but something important——"

"It's always something important, you keep saying that, but I'm not entirely a fool. I know what the real attraction there is—it's Lynn. The way you keep fawning over her at the yacht club and asking her to dance more than me, and——"

"Julie." The edge on Carrick's voice cut her off, and he let the line stay silent for a long moment. "I'll be home soon."

Now, as always, she turned regretful. "Dick, darling, forgive me. I shouldn't have said that. It's just that I miss you so much, and it's dark and I'm all alone here again. Don't be much longer, please, darling?"

"As soon as I can make it," Carrick said, and he turned from the phone with an embarrassed frown. "Where were we? To sum it up——"

"Just a minute," Dan Teague said. The interruption had allowed him to cool himself off a little. "I've been answering questions. Now I'm going to ask one. The last time I asked it I didn't get an answer, but now I'll have to have it. This snatch was pulled for big money, of course, but why should Griff suddenly want one hundred thousand dollars?"

With a gesture Carrick deferred to Spencer Armstead. Lynn saw her father's face darken and she inwardly groaned.

"Very well, chief." The answer came heavily. It was generally known, Spencer Armstead said, that his daughter had inherited a sizeable estate from her mother. Also it was common knowledge that Griff's father had died almost penniless after the collapse of the land boom in the twenties. Griff had never had anything of his own except fairly steady employment—then, after he had quit his job to strike off on his own, a small business as a marine contractor. He had done well enough at it until he had made a serious, crippling mistake.

"Instead of ploughing his earnings back into the business and expanding, as he should have done, he took a reckless plunge—sank all the money he could raise into an option to buy Pelican Key from Bill Rockwood."

Lynn shrank in her chair, remembering this vividly as one of the uncontrollable pressures that had overstrained her marriage to Griff.

"You're already aware of some of this, chief," Spencer Armstead continued, "but the more important parts have been kept a private family matter. Griff and my daughter had lived in this town for years, scarcely noticing each other—socially they were miles apart—and then suddenly Griff began showing what appeared to be a strong romantic interest in her. I suspected his motives. My reason for distrusting him was quite simple. It's all tied in with that starry-eyed pipe-dream of his to develop Pelican Key.

"As his first step, of course, he would have to acquire it —exercise his option—and as always he was in a tearing hurry. Briefly, he found himself completely unable to raise the necessary funds, although Rockwood's price to him was much lower than it might have been to anyone else, for sentimental reasons, because Rockwood and Griff's father had been associates in the original fiasco.

"Once married to Lynn, you see, Griff would share her estate—he might even induce her to sink all her funds into his castles in the air. I faced him with that, openly accused him of it. The result was a scene. Griff denied he was a fortune-hunter, of course. I cornered him—forced him to prove it. I had Dick draw up the proper legal papers and Griff signed them, waiving all rights to Lynn's property for all time."

Lynn closed her eyes. The rift between Griff and her father had never healed. Even before her marriage, this clash had left a scar on their relationship. But it wasn't true that Griff had been greedy for her money. Lynn knew, although her father would never believe it, that Griff had married her for the best, the simplest, and the oldest of reasons.

She looked up again and found Tim Hampden's gaze fixed on her, reproach in his eyes. Was he brooding over Hal again and indirectly blaming her? She thought back to the time when she had broken off her engagement to Tim. If he had any love left for her, it was strained now by bitterness. His eyes seemed to be saying, *If you had married me instead, if you hadn't turned to Griff, none of this would have happened.* . . . Lynn shivered and looked away.

"Lately," Spencer Armstead went on, "Griff has found time running out. His option will expire in a few weeks. He has failed in all his attempts to raise the funds he needs —legitimately. Half the ransom money, one hundred thousand dollars, is considerably short of Rockwood's selling price, but it's still enough to swing the deal. It's as simple as that."

Teague, heavily depressed, was thoughtful for a moment. "But why Lynn as his victim? There are wealthy men with small children near here who might have paid an even bigger ransom."

Spencer Armstead answered with a dour smile. "Chief, it has struck me that there was a certain element of vengefulness and vindictiveness in this crime. Imagine Griff's growing resentment these past few weeks. Imagine the way he has thought back to the origin of his failure. He blames me, of course, because I challenged him, forced him to sign that waiver, and Lynn, too, because her money which might have come into his hands is beyond his reach legally and forever. Thanks chiefly to me, his ridiculously ambitious project began to seem hopeless even to him— unless he could find some desperate, last-minute means of salvaging it. So he thinks to himself how ironical and how deeply gratifying it will be if he can trick us into financing it for him regardless. He'll make it a two-edged achievement—a crushing injury to us and a huge, last-laugh success for himself."

Lynn had listened incredulously, shaking her head. "Dad, it isn't Griff you're talking about. The Griff I know simply isn't capable of that."

"Can you really imagine, my dear, that you know *all* about a man simply because you lived with him one short year? Of course you don't. In the face of the evidence, you must admit that."

The evidence! Lynn thought. The evidence was poison in her mind and she could find no antidote for it.

Teague was speaking. "But how—— If people saw that Griff had suddenly got hold of a big chunk of money, how could he explain it?"

"Like the rest, the answer goes back into his character," Spencer Armstead said. "Griff acts on impulse, before reasoning things through. He simply didn't think it out that far." Lynn's father added: "There's another important angle. I've discussed it with Dick. Lynn and

Griff have been estranged for three months. Suddenly he's trying to forestall a divorce and bring about a reconciliation. Why? It's a precaution, of course. A wife cannot be forced to testify against her husband. Also, Griff would get off easily because we would do our utmost to keep it hushed up—exactly as we are doing."

Teague commented bluntly. "You can't keep it quiet any more, not entirely. Maybe you can still handle the snatch angle, but not the rest—not with a dead man in the case."

The telephone rang again as Lynn gazed hopelessly at their set faces. Spencer Armstead answered the ring and transferred the phone to the chief. Teague listened, spoke in monosyllables, and disconnected. He turned a compassionate look on Lynn before relaying his information to the others.

"That was Doc Elder, pretty upset. It's about Alec Poole. Judge Tyne is hemming and hawing about deciding the cause of death."

Teague was making a face. The responsibilities of the coroner's office required a man of specialized medical training. Judge Tyne's was a purely political appointment. His intentions were as good as his methods were faulty, and his conclusions were sometimes shaped by expediency.

"As of right now," the chief added, "Doc Elder says the coroner's leaning towards calling it accidental death."

They sent puzzled glances at one another.

Spencer Armstead asked bluntly, "But what else——?" and broke off. "Why the devil is Bert Elder upset about that?"

"He didn't explain." Teague went on quietly, "We haven't yet heard Griff's story. Something's going to depend on that. Meanwhile we'd all damned well better do a little hoping—that nothing will happen to make the coroner change his mind."

CHAPTER X

THE WARM YELLOW light of the rising sun found scattered fragments of *Lotus*'s hull floating about Pelican Key. The broken cabin top had washed ashore near the Belle Loma Yacht Club. Four salvaged life-jackets lay drying on the sandy ramp where the shore patrol boat rested. Nothing else was left of *Lotus* except the wreckage strewn on the bottom of the bay.

Waiting alone in the police office, Dan Teague stared out of the door and across the water. Dick Carrick's *Julie* was anchored at the spot where *Lotus* had disappeared. Tim Hampden was aboard, and one of Teague's patrolmen, Frank Anson, an enthusiastic skin-diver, was using an aqua-lung to investigate the broken remains of Griff's boat.

This underwater hunt was another of Carrick's methodical moves, and Griff, of course, was entirely unaware that it was being done. Those men out there were hoping to recover the missing half of the ransom money, or at least to find traces of it. And if they did find it, the case would close even more tightly on the suspected man.

Teague was drinking black coffee, his fourth cup, but there was no stimulation in the stuff this morning. He felt numb with dejection and fatigue. Night before last he had had no rest at all; last night, after leaving the Armstead home, he had managed to hit the sack for three short hours; but hell, he'd learned long ago to get along without much sleep. What had him beat was the way this case was building up so solidly against Griff that there seemed to be no possible way out for the guy. "Open and shut,"

Teague had told Lynn, and that it was—open and shut except for one thin chance, the unlikely possibility that Griff might have a convincing explanation.

Teague rose, opened a door, and walked down the corridor of the cell block. In the first cell a drunken vagrant lay snoring in the bunk. The second and third were empty. Teague paused at the barred door of the fourth and last, frowning at a dark spot on the cement floor. That was where the body of Alec Poole had lain, covered with a sheet, during the night. An hour ago an ambulance from the Park Funeral Chapel had carted it off. Teague had taken a last troubled look at Poole's crushed skull; and the fixed twist of Poole's dead mouth had seemed a mockery.

The chief would never forgive himself for having let Poole dupe him so easily. He had promised himself he would make up for that meat-headed blunder in the only way left to him—by nailing Poole's accomplice.

He opened another door, that of the first-aid room, and stepped in. Griff was lying in the bed, covered with a blanket. As Teague stood frowning at him, Griff rolled his head on the pillow. For a moment there was an odd lack of recognition in his eyes, then a vague perplexity.

"What'm I doing here?"

"Your boat blew up, remember?"

"Sure, but——" Griff felt his face, reddened by the blast; then he discovered that the hand he had lifted was bandaged. Next he moved his other arm and both his legs. Still puzzled, he said, "I'm all right, so what'm I doing here?"

Physically, yes, he was in amazingly good shape. His hard-muscled body had withstood punishment that might have dismembered a softer man. But otherwise—— The outer door of his room was securely locked. Griff had been under guard throughout the night. For all Teague knew,

Griff might continue to be a prisoner from this day on for the rest of his life. . . . He wagged his head, stepped back, and closed the door on Griff.

At his desk again, he went on waiting for Dick Carrick to come. He looked up expectantly as a car stopped in front of the office; but it wasn't Carrick's. The hulking, white-headed man who came marching straight in was Dr. Bertram Elder.

Teague had not talked with Dr. Elder since the phone call to the Armstead home. The doctor was disturbed; the doctor had something upsetting to say, and Teague didn't want to hear it. But no matter; Bert Elder was determined to get it off his chest anyhow.

The doctor stared down at Teague and announced, "Been busy with a difficult delivery or I'd have been here sooner. I want you to understand me, Dan. I'm a good friend of Griff's. So am I a good friend of Spence and Lynn. Also I'm a good doctor and a good citizen who respects his responsibilities. That clear? Now, have you questioned Griff about what happened out there on the bay last night?"

"Not yet."

"Has Judge Tyne made up his mind?"

"Accidental death."

"Accidental hogwash!"

"Judge Tyne decided the damage to Poole's head resulted from the explosion."

"Judge Tyne is an incompetent. He's pussyfooting, afraid to offend position and influence. I have no power to change his hare-brained decision, but I do have a duty. Hell's bells, man, it's obvious. Alec Poole was murdered."

"Judge Tyne thinks he hit his head on a piece of wreckage."

"Nonsense! The man was blown clear, certainly, but, being heavy, he came down while the wreckage was still flying in the air, before there was anything in the water for him to hit. Nor would the water alone smash his skull in like that. He was struck from above, two powerful blows. *Two* blows, hear me?—one almost on top of the other but not quite, with some sort of weapon that was cylindrical in shape. It could have been done before the boat blew up or——"

"Cylindrical?" Teague was gazing at the doctor bleakly. "You could tell that?"

"By the shape of the fractures, naturally, the imprints. A blind man could see it."

"And the coroner is worse than blind? Did you argue this out with him?"

"You can't argue with a fool who won't listen."

Teague drew a deep breath. "You realize—if he had agreed with you—what this would mean for Griff?"

"Certainly I realize it. But understand me again. I'm not accusing anyone. Liking Griff as much as I do, I can't believe he's guilty of murdering that man." In the intensity of his conviction, Dr. Elder had bent low over the desk, pushing his face towards Teague's. Now he straightened indignantly. "I am simply stating my considered medical opinion that the man was murdered—by a person or persons unknown."

Teague said evenly, "Accidental death, doctor. The certificate, duly signed by Acting Coroner Tyne, makes it official and final—unless you intend to raise a stink about it."

"I have no intention whatever of breathing a word of this to anyone else. Good day, chief."

Dr. Elder marched out of the office and back to his car. As the doctor drove off, Teague sat growling to himself. This case wasn't a big enough headache already. It wasn't tough enough for him to have to pin a kidnapping rap on Griff; no, the good doctor had to insist dutifully and righteously and loudly upon bringing murder into it as well. . . . The worst of it was that Teague hadn't needed this. On the basis of his own examination of Poole's body, made hours ago, he had reached the same conclusion.

Squirming in his chair, Teague damned his job and went on damning it until another car stopped. This time it was the expected one, Carrick's. The chief watched grimly while Carrick alighted, carrying a black leather-covered case and a long, coiled extension-cord. Carrick made a quiet entrance, aiming an inquisitive look at the chief, and Teague nodded. *It's okay now; he's awake.*

Teague indicated an electrical outlet in the wall. Carrick sank the plug of the extension-cord into it. Without speaking, the chief led the way down the corridor of the cell block. Making as few sounds as possible, and still carrying the case by its handle, Carrick paid out the cord as he followed. Inside the fourth cell he placed the tape recorder on the bunk. For the next few minutes he was busy with his preparations, perching the microphone carefully on the sill of a louver high in the wall, adjusting the earphones, checking the recording level. Finishing, he raised an expectant look at Teague. *We're all set; go to it.*

Sick-hearted, Teague went back into the first-aid room.

Griff had thrown off the sheet and pushed himself to a sitting position on the edge of the bed. He tried to stand, and a whirl of dizziness overwhelmed him. When it cleared he found himself flat on his back again and a blurred Dan Teague bending over him.

"What did you want to do that for?" the chief said. "You're not going anywhere."

Griff squinted, trying to bring him into focus. That was Dan Teague's face all right, but it wasn't his voice. It seemed to echo, strangely hard and distant, as in a cavern. It brought a new confusion to Griff, a sense that in some way he must have got himself in wrong with Teague—but he couldn't think how.

"Feel like talking?"

Griff blinked at him. Feel like talking about what? Oh, the boat. Teague wanted to know how come his boat had exploded. Griff opened his mouth to answer, then closed it again, frowning in puzzlement. Why *had* it blown up? He remembered taking *Lotus* out. He remembered being hurled by a terrific blast and finding himself threshing about in the black water. But in between—— It was the beginning and the end of a bad dream, with the middle part missing.

"Is she gone?" Griff asked.

"Total loss. She was insured, wasn't she?"

The answer came to him from an earlier, easily remembered period. "No. When renewal time came—— Short of money, let it lapse." He looked startled. "Total loss?"

Teague nodded, studying him as if he were some unfamiliar kind of bug. "Go on, tell me about it."

Griff recalled vividly the instant of violence. Like the split-second brilliance of a flash bulb, this sharp sense of alarm had photographed it on his mind. "I shouldn't have dropped the wrench. It made a big spark." He stopped, rubbing his forehead with his gauze-gloved hand. Again he could see the white-hot spark flying out, but before and after that—— His memory was a black rag, torn and full of holes.

"Griff, do you know what you're talking about?"

"Sure I do."

"I'm trying to find out why your boat blew up. Do you understand?"

"Sure I do. I told you. The wrench—knocked loose from my hand."

"Knocked loose how?"

"I think something—some*body* hit me."

Teague's eyes sharpened at him. "Somebody you'd taken aboard your boat?"

"No. I hadn't taken anybody aboard."

"If somebody hit you, as you say, that person had to be in your boat."

"I guess so. Sure. I got hit. That's why I dropped the wrench. I got hit damn hard."

"This was just before the boat blew up?"

"The wrench fell on the storage battery. It seemed to take a long time falling. Couldn't think of anything else—waited a long time for it to land. But—when everything seemed to be happening so fast——"

"Somebody was on your boat, Griff?" Teague persisted. "Who was it?"

"I couldn't see—didn't have time——"

"Why did he hit you?"

The reason had something to do with something else. Griff almost had it, but not quite.

"Griff, listen. Is your mind clear enough to answer these questions?"

Griff had never before felt at so great a loss. It was a weakness, strange to him; he was chagrined and ashamed to admit it. "I'm all right," he said.

"Go on with it, then."

"Go on? From where?"

"From the beginning. I was there on your pier last night when you put out. It was beginning to get dark. You were alone in your boat then, remember?"

"Sure I remember," Griff insisted. "Alone, heading over to the cottage—spend the night."

"You were a mile or so from the cove on Pelican Key when the Coast Guard boat passed you."

"Sure, that's right."

"Then?"

Blankness.

"You were heading over to Pelican Key and you were about a mile offshore, Griff, when your boat blew up. That clear?"

"Sure."

"I want to know why it happened."

Why? Griff's mind felt its way backward little by little. 'I'm beginning to remember now. I smelt gas. Opened the hatch—— Somebody'd been below, down there in the engine compartment, bumping around. In the dark maybe—knocked the safety cover off the storage battery—leaned against the fuel line and bent it so it sprang a leak. That's the way I figured it anyhow. So I went below and started to fix it and——"

Griff was lost in the blackness again.

"You say somebody hit you. When?"

"It must've been just about then."

"Who did that?"

"I told you, Dan, I couldn't see."

"It was Alec Poole, wasn't it?"

"Who?"

"Where did you pick up Alec Poole?"

Griff stared at Teague. "Didn't pick up anybody."

Teague's eyes hardened. "Griff, once before in this case I was played for a fool. I damned well won't let it happen again."

Perplexed, silent, Griff wondered what Teague meant by that.

"I know you were alone when you put out in your boat. I know Poole was in your boat when she blew up. You——"

"He was?"

"Damned right he was! You must have taken him aboard at some point in between. Where was it—at the pier of the Azalea Motel?"

Griff stiffened himself against the pressure. "Didn't pick

up anybody anywhere," he said stubbornly. Then a thought struck him—it seemed brilliant. "Bob Sage can tell you. He saw me. Nobody else aboard."

"Because Poole was hiding in the cabin then?"

Griff's confusion was growing. What was Teague getting at? Why was he being questioned like this? His boat was gone—a total loss, no insurance, a serious thing—so why must Teague keep poking at him about somebody named—what was it?—Poole.

"I don't know anybody named Poole," Griff said flatly.

He saw the colour of anger in Teague's face and it bothered him; he couldn't account for it.

"Didn't you hear me, Griff? Poole was with you when your boat blew up. We *know* that."

Griff felt overpowered by the force of Teague's conviction. Teague must be right, he thought; Teague was leaving him no room to doubt this. But—— "Poole? How did he get aboard? What did he want?"

"Knock it off, Griff!" At the very moment when Griff needed Teague's help the most, the chief turned more impatient, his voice harsher. "You said you remember, you said your mind's clear. Now you're putting on an act, trying to play dumb. Knock it off!"

It startled Griff and added to his bewilderment. Teague thought he was faking; that was why Teague was sore. Faking? Why should he? What did Teague think he was trying to hide?

"Lying about that part——" the chief said disgustedly. "Hell, you've got a lot of breath to waste. You're only making it rougher for yourself."

Lying? Griff resented that. He was trying his level best to get at the elusive truth, to tell it straight. If Teague would just give him a little more time—if Teague would just wait until he got things properly arranged in his mind——

"Make *what* rougher?" Griff asked suddenly.

Teague sat there cold-faced. "All right, Griff. If you want it the hard way, that's the way you'll get it."

Now what did that mean? . . . Wait a minute. Poole? Alec Poole? Belatedly the name turned on a light. Poole was that odd ball who had the boat called *Playmate*. No, *Playgirl*. Sure, Griff had seen him here and there around town—but why did Teague want to make something big of that? Griff was about to correct himself, to admit he knew who Poole was, when Teague spoke again and threw him off the track.

"You hit your head, you said. Or somebody slugged you. Which was it?"

"I told you before, Dan——" This was the emptiest cranny of Griff's memory. He kept remembering the spark, the shooting spark so brilliant in the surrounding darkness. He had a cloudy feeling the spark was only one of many things that had happened all together, and he couldn't sort them over or bring them apart. "I told you before, I think somebody rocked me with a terrific one, but I couldn't see."

"You couldn't have been slugged if nobody else was aboard. If you were slugged, it had to be Alec Poole who did it. So when and how did Poole get in your boat?"

Griff felt he could explain it somehow. He had the answer somewhere. If only Teague would give him a chance to fish deep into all the dark pockets of his mind——

"It was the other way around, wasn't it? Poole didn't slug you. *You* slugged *him*."

"No!" What was the matter with Dan Teague? Why did he insist on misunderstanding things? "I was below, in the engine compartment, and I was just straightening up——" Griff stopped. "Why did you say that? Why should I? I had no reason—— I didn't even know he was there—if he was."

The chief sat back, his mouth thinned. "All right, go on. What's the rest of it?"

The rest? Yes—there was more. It went back a little in time. While he was ducked down in the engine compartment, working on the fuel line, something else had happened, something he wanted to tell Teague about. . . . Griff shook his head. He couldn't quite reach it.

"That—that's all."

"Not quite." The chief leaned tensely toward him again. "Where'd you get that package?"

A far-away candle flame flickered. "Package——?"

Teague's mouth worked with repressed fury. Faking, lying—the chief thought he was trying in every way possible to evade the truth.

"Don't give me that blank look, Griff! You know damned well what I'm talking about. You had a package —a package wrapped in plastic film and sealed—hidden in your boat. Don't try to deny that part either. I found it floating with the wreckage. Now answer that question. *Where'd you get it?*"

Griff went tightly on the defensive. Teague's mention of the package had brought it back as the dimmest sort of image. Much clearer was the fact that, no matter what else it might mean, it was packed with serious trouble for him. Hidden on his boat?—yes, it had been, but Griff couldn't explain that, and Teague's manner had warned him clearly enough that to admit it would be dangerous. . . . Griff was dizzy again—bone-tired, sick with returning weakness. He didn't want to answer any more questions.

"Don't know anything about—a package."

Teague stood. Rearing over him, Teague looked huge and darkly menacing, like a storm cloud about to burst.

"Let's see if I've got this story of yours straight. There

was a fuel leak. You went down into the engine compartment to fix it. When you straightened up you hit your
head. Either that or somebody socked you. But if somebody did hit you, you don't know who it was, and anyhow
you hadn't taken anybody else aboard. You dropped a
wrench on the battery and a spark set off the explosion.
That right?"

Griff gazed up at him hopelessly.

"You're not acquainted with Alec Poole," the chief
added in a tone of scorn, "and you don't remember a
damn thing about any package."

Griff had only one more thing to say. A question.
"Dan——" He felt a vast loneliness as he asked it. "Dan,
does Lynn know what happened?"

At that Teague's self-control was almost shattered. He
closed one fist white-hard; he turned and banged out.

Griff lay inert, yielding his senses to a flooding greyness.
He felt a sad sense of loss. Without understanding why,
he knew that Dan Teague's friendship with him had
ended.

CHAPTER XI

Dick Carrick had brought the tape recorder directly
to the Armstead home. Chief Teague, he had told Lynn
and her father, had gone to the Azalea Motel to question
Vina Daly; and Tim Hampden, aboard *Julie*, was still
supervising the underwater search for *Lotus*'s wreckage.
Now they were hearing Teague's questions and Griff's
stumbling answers played back for the second time.

"Griff, do you understand?"

"Sure I do."

"*Is your mind clear?*"

"*I'm all right. . . . Sure I remember.*"

"He had to insist on it," Spencer Armstead said, "—had to try his best to make it stick."

Lynn's father was moving about behind her chair, restless with a growing indignation. Carrick stood beside the instrument, listening with his professional mind, analysing this vulnerable testimony. The tape passing from reel to reel was like a belt of abrasive wearing against Lynn's loyalty and hopefulness.

"*Didn't pick up anybody anywhere. . . . I don't know anybody named Poole. . . . Don't know anything about a package.*"

"Lies," Spencer Armstead asserted. "Outright lies!"

Lynn pitied Griff. This instrument, in its very faithfulness to reality, was a frightening and cruel thing—all Griff's confusions and evasions were repeated with a relentless sameness. At the touch of a switch he could be made to discredit himself out of his own mouth over and over, and every reiteration would strengthen the probability of his guilt.

Her eyes stinging, she listened for his final murmured words.

"*Dan—— Dan, does Lynn know what happened?*"

"That was his sly way of asking whether Lynn knows he did this damnably outrageous thing to her," Spencer Armstead said. "If she does, he can't hope to persuade her to drop the divorce action—he's lost her as a means of self-protection."

Then, from the loud-speaker, the wrathful slam of a door—the sound of Dan Teague's denouncement.

Carrick switched off the recorder and for a moment the room was still. Lynn felt it had been unfair to Griff to question him so soon, without a doctor's consent. She had phoned Bertram Elder last night to inquire concerning Griff, and Dr. Bert had said then that a temporary blank-

118

ing-out of memory, complete or partial, was symptomatic of concussion.

"Granted, he was badly shaken up," Lynn's father said, as if reading her thoughts. "Given more time he might have cooked up something more convincing. This flimsy fabrication was the best he could do in his condition—fortunately for us."

Lynn wanted desperately to believe Griff had told the truth, or had tried to tell it as clearly as he could, yet she realized that in justice to her father and herself she could not shut her eyes to the refuting facts.

Poole *had* been aboard Griff's boat. One or the other of them, or both, *had* been in possession of at least half the ransom money. Lynn could not doubt that this move had been part of the kidnappers' master plan, an action taken in secrecy under cover of darkness, and Griff *had* participated in it. The explosion aboard *Lotus* had disrupted and exposed it, and Griff, finding himself literally hurled into a welter of incriminating circumstances, had tried feebly to deny the undeniable.

"Lynn," Carrick said quietly, "you realize, don't you, that you're the key to this whole case?"

A key, Lynn thought, gazing at him uneasily, was a two-way thing. It could open a prison cell. The same key could lock it inescapably.

"With Poole dead, and Hal Hampden still unconscious and weakening, you're the only one of the three victims in this case who can speak out. A great deal will rest on what you believe and what you say."

"Yes."

"You could, if you wished—and if it came to this—testify on the witness-stand that Griff did not take part in the kidnapping. You could swear under oath, 'No, I'm completely convinced that neither of those two men was my husband'—and our case would collapse. But as the

119

matter stands now, Lynn, could you honourably **do** that?"

She thought of the moment yesterday afternoon when, wavering at the head of the stairs, she had listened to Griff unconsciously whistling to himself—the same fragmentary tune she had heard whistled by the man walking furtively about outside the hide-out. The certainty had pierced her then that this man—who had not been searching for her, who had made no move at all towards helping her— actually was Griff. She was still certain of it; she could account for his presence and his actions in only one way— Griff *had* been one of that criminal pair. Her father and Dick Carrick, had they known this, would have seized on it as the blackest of all the evidence against Griff. She hadn't told them, hadn't brought herself to that point of painful finality.

"*I'm completely convinced that neither of those two men was my husband*"—could she say that? Say it—Dick Carrick's word—honourably?

"No," Lynn answered. "I couldn't. Not now."

Carrick smiled and Lynn's father put his hand gratefully on her shoulder.

"There's one decisive point we can't get around, Lynn," Carrick said. "There's nothing, nothing at all to point to anyone other than Griff, and Poole as his accomplice."

"Nothing."

"Poole was the man you called the rough one. It was Poole who gave Hal that brutal beating, who later struck you with his fist. They must have used Poole's boat for their trips to and from the hide-out—until last night, when they used Griff's instead, because they could be sure the Coast Guard would pass it without bothering to search it."

"They had the money aboard," Lynn admitted reluctantly. "At least half the money."

"The chief of police had been checking up on Poole, and

that must have scared him," Carrick said. "If Poole had had his half of the ransom cached somewhere nearby, he'd naturally want to get it farther out of Dan's reach in a hurry. It's thoroughly reasonable to assume their purpose last night was to sneak Poole's share of the money, if not both halves, over to a safer hiding-place on one of the Keys."

"And something went wrong. The accident—the explosion——"

Spencer Armstead said bluntly, "I cannot believe the explosion was accidental. Poole had with him one hundred thousand dollars in cash. He probably intended to bury it somewhere deep in the jungle, or on one of the island beaches. As a safeguard he would insist on going ashore alone so that not even Griff would know just where he'd hidden it. Once he'd done that, his money would be beyond Griff's reach—or, at best, finding it would be a hard, time-consuming job. Picture the situation, Lynn. There they were, far out on the water, in the dark, and all Griff needed was to catch Poole off guard for a few seconds. Dog eat dog—one crook double-crossing another, Griff getting all the money for himself."

Carrick went on. "A *delayed* explosion, Lynn—tricky, but not too hard to arrange. If Griff had it rigged that way, he must have intended to go overboard with the package and be clear of the boat by the time the explosion occurred. He could swim to Pelican Key unnoticed and hide the money quickly in a temporary place. Afterwards he would have no trouble explaining how Poole happened to be in his boat because, up to that time, Poole was entirely in the clear."

"Judge Tyne played straight into Griff's hands," Spencer Armstead said contemptuously, "—accepted the appearance of an accident in just the way Griff had planned it."

"But as you said, Lynn, something went wrong, badly so. Griff's timing was off. The blast let go too soon and Griff himself was caught in it."

They were adding evil to evil—they believed there was no limit to Griff's viciousness.

Carrick saw Lynn's heartache and spoke sympathetically. "This is all supposition, let's admit that. It logically explains what happened, although we can't prove it."

Lynn's father turned to him. "Perhaps not, Dick, but neither can we doubt it. Our evidence points to no one else, to no other conclusion."

Lynn was astonished to see Carrick shaking his head.

"Actually, Spence, this case shapes up as a peculiar yes-and-no thing. Looking at it from the viewpoint of a defence attorney, I think Griff would have a fifty-fifty chance of getting off."

"What? How can you say that?"

"Take Poole's part in it, for example. He's beyond confessing. Lynn can't identify him, not now. Griff has denied knowing him. There was nothing to show complicity on Poole's part, and there were no suspicious contacts between him and Griff, so far as we know, until last night."

"Griff and Poole were pulled out of the water at the same spot and at the same time," Spencer Armstead reminded him with gruff impatience. "Most certainly that shows they were accomplices."

"It's circumstantial, Spence—not conclusive proof they were both in *Lotus* when she blew up. There's no eye-witness to testify they were in Griff's boat together. On the contrary, Dan saw Griff putting out alone, and Bob Sage saw him still alone close to the spot where the explosion occurred. Or, take the package of money found floating among the wreckage. Who can say positively where it came from? There's no direct evidence to place it unquestionably in Griff's possession, or even to show he had knowledge of it. Griff's attorney could argue any one of several other possible explanations—he could riddle the prosecution's case with doubt, and reasonable doubt is the basic, deciding factor.''

Spencer Armstead was growing angry. "This is preposterous! Every piece of evidence points to Griff as the instigator, and to no one else—including the telephone call. You yourself saw him making the call—you timed it. *That* certainly can't be explained away.''

"Consider, Spence. I did see Griff putting through a phone call at 1.13 a.m., and at 1.13 a.m. you received a message from one of the kidnappers. It couldn't be a coincidence—the chances against it are astronomical. Yet a fighting defence attorney could make it seem to be one—he could argue that there are sixty or seventy thousand telephones operating through the Palmport exchange, and he could easily establish the fact that at that same moment other phones were in use—twenty, fifty, a hundred, even more. Can we prove beyond a reasonable doubt that the call received here at one-thirteen did not come from one of those many other phones? No, not possibly.''

"You're splitting hairs, Dick. Legal trickery can't alter the facts. The man who made that phone call said, 'That's better, stay alone there.' He knew you and Tim had left this house a few minutes earlier—as Griff did.''

Lynn's mind grasped at that fact, held it, turned it over. It was one of the most telling points against Griff, yet it was vaguely puzzling. Was there a flaw hidden in it somewhere? . . . Distracted by Carrick, she let it go. Carrick was brushing aside her father's argument, speaking with surprising fire.

"Damn it all, Spence, I'm not saying Griff is innocent. I'm sure he's not. No amount of money could induce me to defend him in court. But as I've told you before, moral certainty is not enough. Nor is personal bias. I've simply tried to show you that our case is weak—seriously so."

Spencer Armstead answered that with a wrathful outburst. Who else but Griff *could* be the perpetrator? He was palpably guilty of a whole series of barbarous criminal acts. Think of it!—the almost fatal assault on Hal Hampden, Lynn's terror, the privations and suffering forced on her, the brutal blow smashing into her blindness—the treachery, the basest sort of treachery against his own wife and against his partner in crime as well. Incredible that this—this monster should stand half a chance of going unpunished!

Lynn felt a deep elemental ache. "This monster" was her husband, her baby his child. Would Spencer Armstead have tempered his rage if he had known? . . . No. She shook her head and closed her eyes against tears.

"Spence," Carrick said placatingly when the storm had subsided, "the important question is how to add strength to our case. What weapons can we use against Griff? Pressure. Attritions. That's all. Griff is tough, obstinate —with so much at stake he'll resist his hardest. He won't be worn down, not by you or me or Dan Teague or all of us working together." Carrick paused. "But like most of us, he has an Achilles heel, a soft spot."

A hint of challenge in Carrick's voice caused Lynn to look up. Carrick was quietly estimating her.

"We need help, help of a special kind. Help from you, Lynn."

She sensed that this was something her father and Carrick had already discussed and agreed upon. They wanted her to help them clinch the question of Griff's guilt! The suggestion staggered her, left her too dazed to answer.

A sound at the front door interrupted. Tim Hampden stepped in. His face was pink with new sunburn from his hours on the bay and almost sullen with fatigue.

"Nothing," he reported, in answer to their questioning looks. "No package. Not a single loose bill. No trace of the money at all."

Spencer Armstead frowned at that, but Carrick's eyes brightened.

"It seems to confirm our reconstruction of what happened last night," the lawyer said. "Griff and Poole had only half the ransom aboard—Poole's share. Griff must have left his half hidden in its own place, probably somewhere here in Belle Loma." He was estimating Lynn again. "One hundred thousand dollars—money belonging to your father. It's of no value to Griff now—he won't dare to use it—and Spence can ill afford to lose it."

Lynn responded with a question she could not avoid. "What do you want me to do?"

"See Griff."

"Simply see him?"

"He's reaching for a reconciliation with you, Lynn. Regardless of his reason, it's important to him. You could easily—well, let him feel encouraged."

"I see." She did not try to hide her resentment and reproach. "You mean play him along—take advantage of him."

Spencer Armstead said bluntly, "And why not? He exploited you, and me as well, cruelly and criminally. Fight fire with fire!"

"I should bait him, try to trick him into betraying himself. Is that what you're asking me to do?"

"If Griff falls into a trap," Spencer Armstead said hotly, "it will be because he's guilty, and he'll deserve the consequences. I don't understand you, Lynn! Can you—you, one of his victims—can you possibly feel you owe him any forgiveness whatever?"

She remembered her interminable imprisonment, her

loathing for both her captors. "No. Not if he's really guilty."

"Then, Lynn," Carrick said, "let's put it this way. You appreciate your responsibility to your father—there's no need to dwell on that. But you also owe something highly important to yourself. You ought to come through all this with no doubt left in your mind, not a shadow of a doubt one way or the other. *Complete* certainty, Lynn."

"Yes."

"No one else can give that to you. You'll have to go after it on your own. And the only source is Griff himself."

Lynn gazed at the drawn face of her father, the eyes so deeply hurt by her hesitation, and knew she could not refuse him.

"You won't even need to approach Griff," Carrick added. "In a natural, casual way you can let him come to you. Let him talk, and listen carefully to what he says. Simply that."

With surprise and a new lift of hopefulness she realized she did not wish to refuse. She hadn't been near Griff to look into his face and see him again for herself. What would she see—his true face or a mask of deceit? Who would she find—the evildoer her father thought him to be or a man to whom she could return her trust? She had not entirely lost it. "He's incapable of all this," she had said; "this isn't the Griff I know," and "Something's wrong, dreadfully wrong." She could still believe that and hope to find it still true. . . . Now that her decision was made, the repellent demand had become an opportunity for Griff, one which she alone could give him.

Lynn stood. "First I want to see Alec Poole's girl."

Carrick looked astonished, but he nodded. "I'll take you to her as soon as——"

"I want to see her alone," Lynn said. "And now."

She stopped her open convertible in the courtyard of the Azalea Motel alongside Dan Teague's official car. The chief himself was not in sight. A white-haired, ruddy-faced man inside the cubicle of an office—Mr. Clane, the owner—watched her uneasily from his desk chair as she alighted. She didn't need to ask him for the number of Vina Daly's room. Voices audible through the open jalousies led her to it—first a woman's raised on a wailing note of complaint.

"You stop this now, you big snoopy bully! Alec's dead. Can't you let him alone?"

The masculine rumble was Dan Teague's. Then Vina Daly again, thinly screeching.

"No, I said! Put me in jail, I don't care. You can't make me talk about Alec. Twenty times I've told you I won't do it. You better get the hell out of here!"

Lynn was near the door when it opened. Teague's forehead was sweating, his mouth thinned with exasperation. He shook his head at Lynn—*hopeless!* Looking in, she saw Vina Daly slumped back in a chair, staring hypnotically at the wall. Barefoot and bare-shouldered, in green shorts and a white tube-top, a tall empty glass in one hand, her hair mussed, her lipstick smeared off—a woman lost in desolation.

Lynn's glance at the chief said, *Let me try*, and without commenting he strode off. She waited outside until he was starting away in the police sedan, then went in quietly. Vina did not notice her.

"You big nosey jerk," Vina said to the officer who was no longer there. "Can't let people alone. Not even dead people. I got things to say all right, but not to you."

Lynn touched her hand. Vina lifted her colourless face and narrowed her eyes.

"What're *you* doing here?"

"I'm——"

"I know who you are." Vina's voice was low and taut with bitterness. "I hate you."

"But—why?"

"Because I hate *him*." Vina stiffened to her bare feet. "I hate everything about him. Alec wouldn't be dead if it wasn't for him."

"Griff?" Lynn was shaken. "You can't really believe that."

"Alec was going to marry me. All these years he wouldn't. Over and over I asked him to marry me and he'd just laugh." Vina was speaking through a pent-in fury. "I didn't *have* to marry him. I never got pregnant by him. Making it *right*—I didn't care anything about that. I just wanted to be married to Alec, that was all. Finally, just last week, he said all right. And now he's dead."

"I'm so sorry——"

"That's what *your* man did to *my* man." It was hardly more than a whisper, a vehemently hostile confidence.

"No, Vina, I'm sure you're wrong about——"

"Soon, Alec said. As soon as he'd wrapped up this certain job he was working on. He'd be loaded with dough then, he said. I didn't care about money. I had enough for both of us. But Alec'd got himself into this big thing, he wanted to get it made for himself." Vina choked on her resentment. "If it wasn't for that he wouldn't be dead."

Lynn asked carefully, "What was he doing, Vina?"

"He never told me anything. But I know it wasn't Alec's idea. He let himself get hooked into it. Once when he was drunk he let something slip. This partner of his, he said, this smart operator he was in it with had to raise a lot of money in a hurry to put into a big land deal."

Lynn's breath stopped for a moment. "What kind of a big land deal? Where?"

"Here. Something about an island—some kind of option on it—Pelican Key."

"Did he tell you this—this partner's name?" Lynn put both her hands on Vina's shoulders. "Did he say definitely it was Griff? *Did he?*"

"He didn't need to say that. I saw who he'd been talking to. Once over on Pelican Key, once out on the bay, other places too, real confidential-like, real careful I wouldn't hear anything. They thought I didn't know they were up to something, but I did. Every single time it was this Griff of yours."

"You've got to be sure of this. Griff wasn't the only one Alec talked to like that. Who else did you see with Alec?"

"Alec should have listened to me, but he wouldn't. He worried me so."

"Vina! There had to be another man, someone besides Griff. Think back. Try to——"

"Nobody else. *Never* anybody else. Just this Griff of yours. If it wasn't for him, him and his big-money deals, Alec wouldn't be dead."

Vina twisted herself free of Lynn's hands; she dropped herself to the bed and lay still, starkly dry-eyed.

"That two-faced Griff of yours!—he ought to get it where it really hurts for what he did. But I don't care. It wouldn't bring Alec back. Most of all I don't want people to know Alec let himself get sucked in by that sneaky crooked bastard."

Lynn left the room quickly, her cheeks stiff and cold. Had anyone overheard? No; no one was near. Vina had screeched at Dan Teague in defence of Alec Poole, revealing nothing; but to Lynn she had spoken in a manner of shared secrecy, and her very quietness had carried crushing force. Only Vina's curious personal code, her faithfulness to a dead unworthy lover, had saved Griff from total condemnation.

CHAPTER XII

At this time of the afternoon the first-aid room was a hot-box. The tropical sun blazed in the barred windows and reflected on the hospital-white walls and white enamelled cabinets, filling it with inescapable glare. Griff had thrown the sheet aside, with little relief; the air was like a sticky liquid coating his naked body.

All day he had been left alone here. Pointedly and ominously, Dan Teague had not returned since their clash early this morning. At noon, when Frank Anson had brought a bowl of hot bean-soup, Griff had tried a few questions, but Anson, in and out quickly, had ducked them: "Wouldn't know—better see Dan about it." Afterwards, the soup eaten, feeling stronger, Griff had decided he'd had enough of this silent treatment—he'd face Teague and find out, here and now, where he stood.

The locked door had stopped him. He had knocked and called Teague's name. The chief had not answered; no one had come.

Hours of solitude had stimulated Griff's thinking. Lying with his eyes closed, resisting the mounting oppressiveness of the heat, he had persistently explored the labyrinth of his memory. Groping back and forth, he had tracked light into most of its turnings, but there was still one great dark cavern through which he could not find his way.

Those turbulent minutes immediately following the explosion—— While he was floundering in the black water, something had happened that had been as frightening and incredible as a nightmare. Without knowing quite why, Griff felt it was important to him—vitally important that he recall it. No one else could tell him what it was; he had experienced it in a moment of terrible aloneness. . . . No use trying again; he couldn't bring it back. The harder he strained towards it, the farther it slipped away.

Yet in another sense, Griff realized, it wasn't important at all. No matter if he had remembered everything, every single detail with perfect clarity, Dan Teague wouldn't have believed him.

Impulsively Griff pushed himself up from the cot. He was through taking it lying down. He had his legs back now; he had his hands to work with; he could get at this crazy business, take hold of it and begin clearing it up. He rapped his knuckles hard on the bolted door. "Dan! . . . Hey, Dan! . . ." As before, the chief didn't answer; no one came.

Griff tried the other way out, the entrance facing Nineteenth Street. It, too, was fastened as immovably as the door of a convict's cell. Bolts, bars!—why? If Dan Teague had a good reason for keeping him under lock and key, he damned well had a right to hear what it was. Teague would have to come back sooner or later, and then it would be cards on the table—either that or there'd be one hell of a blow-up.

Circling the room, strengthened by a rebellious impatience, Griff stripped the bandages off his hands and threw them aside. He found a small electric fan sitting on a wall-bracket and switched it on. It began a frantic buzzing and wagging that scarcely stirred the sultry air. Next, in a curtained-off corner, he found his clothes, dry but shapelessly wrinkled. He put them on. He was getting into his loafers, about to turn to the inner door again, when it swung open.

Dr. Bertram Elder stopped just inside with a surprised "Ha?" Griff braced himself as Dan Teague followed.

The doctor came on and with one big paw on Griff's

chest backed him to a chair placed against the wall. Griff submitted wordlessly while Dr. Elder took his pulse, listened to his heartbeat, and flashed a light in his eyes. "Slow," the doctor muttered; "still a little slow but otherwise—*ha!*"

All the while Griff kept a frown on Teague. The chief's look was neither friendly nor hostile, but hard with a quality of concealment that stirred misgivings in Griff and put him on his guard. *Better watch this cop*, he warned himself. *He's wound up, ready to pitch a fast one. Better pitch first.*

"You think Alec Poole and I pulled off some kind of a crooked deal together," Griff said abruptly. "In fact, you're damned sure of it."

"Well, Griff—— I *was sure.*"

He grasped at Teague's answer. "What do you mean by that—you've changed your mind?"

"I've had time to check and think it over. Lacking evidence to the contrary, we'll have to take your word for what happened."

"This morning you weren't willing to take my word for anything. You seemed to have evidence then—at least you asked me about a package of some kind. What about that?"

"Well—— I'm still not sure just how to figure that item, Griff. We're keeping the lid on and trying to find out if——"

Griff broke in. "What was in the package, Dan?"

Teague didn't like this abrupt turnabout—finding himself suddenly on the answering end. "Can't tell you about that. It's probably hot. Might be tied in with—well, maybe a robbery somewhere. We're investigating."

"Money," Griff said. "How much money?"

Teague shook his head.

"Where did it come from? Who does it belong to?"

"We're looking into it," Teague said shortly.

"This robbery, or whatever it was—did Alec Poole **do** it?"

"We're checking."

"Did he pull it off single-handed?"

"I doubt it." Teague glared. He had slipped, had said a little too much. "Lay off, Griff. If you had nothing to do with Poole or the package, as you said, this can't be of any importance to you."

Not important? Griff felt that Teague had shut him off from information that might have helped them both. Well, hell, that was a game two could play. Having denied all knowledge of the package, Griff would gain nothing by spilling it now.

"A bundle of hot money," he said, watching Teague carefully. "One? That was it—only that one?"

"One was all we found."

Griff knew the chief had been feeding him a series of evasions, but this answer rang true. He could accept it even though it confused him. There had been *two* packages. After removing the nearest from its hiding-place, Griff had decided to leave the second where it was. Straightening from the engine compartment, he had turned to the package he had placed on the deck and had seen a hand closed on it—a hand lifting it, then pitching it far overboard.

Overboard! Why? . . . Griff had no answer, but he did have a clear mental image of that rapidly moving hand.

"I told you this morning, Dan—— Just before the explosion somebody slugged me."

"Or else you hit your head."

"You think I could imagine that—getting slugged?"

"Possibly. You were in a state of shock afterwards, pretty mixed-up. You're probably remembering the explosion itself."

This was a surprising change of face, Griff thought—the

133

way Teague had turned so charitable. He distrusted it, but he didn't argue. The question bothering Griff was this: Which of the two packages was the one Teague had found?

Griff suspected it was the other one which he had left wired in position—it must have stayed there until the shattering of the deck had freed it. Then what had become of the first, the one Griff had seen flying off into the darkness? . . . This was the same darkness that remained in his mind, the one void he still could not fill.

"One thing I don't get," Griff said. "First thing this morning you started hammering at me. Why didn't you go to work on Poole instead?"

Dr. Elder had been a silent listener. At this he turned an astonished glance on the chief, then lowered his bristly eyebrows at Griff. "You don't know? Well, he's dead, that's the first thing about Poole."

"Dead?"

"As dead as they come. Accident, the coroner says. Decided that last night."

Griff absorbed it quickly, still frowning at Teague. "Accident?"

Teague said casually—*too* casually, "That's a break for everybody concerned. The D.A. was ready to move in. The FBI asked some questions. Nothing to be done, I told 'em. There won't even be an inquest. Makes it easier all around."

"Accident," Griff repeated. "You knew this morning. But still you put me on the grill about it."

Teague's gesture was meant to be disarming, Griff imagined. "Just routine. The way I found his body in the bay where your tub went up—hell, Griff, I had to look into that from every angle. You claim you didn't even know Poole, and that——"

"I did know him slightly." Griff put in, watching

Teague. "I remember now, running into him a couple of times. A few days ago, for instance, on my pier. He was looking *Lotus* over—seemed pretty interested in her for some reason. I wondered why."

"He had time to kill—loafed around town a lot, poking his nose in where he wasn't wanted and had no business. Trouble-prone, an odd streak in him—self-destructiveness. I remember one time finding him asleep on the sea wall—one roll in the wrong direction and he'd have fallen smack on to those sharp-edged rocks and probably drowned. We can't be sure, but it could have been that again last night, or maybe he stumbled off a pier, blind drunk, and hit his head on something. Body floated on the tide—after dark, nobody noticed until the explosion brought all those boats out. So, the way he turned up dead there—a coincidence, that's all."

Dr. Elder was scowling at Teague. He uttered a bursting sound of disgust—"*Phah!*"—caught up his medicine-case, and strode straight out of the room. The bang of the door said emphatically, *I wash my hands of this humbuggery!*

Griff felt he knew the reason behind the doctor's indignation. The explanation Teague had offered not only assumed too much, it was also a deliberate distortion of facts. This Teague, who had been such a tough-minded cop this morning, was talking out of the other side of his mouth, and for a purpose—without believing a word he said. Now it was Griff's turn to be tough-minded. Poole's dead body had been found there among the wreckage just by chance? No. Griff knew it had not been a coincidence.

It *was* Poole who had come aboard *Lotus* only a minute or two before the explosion. How? This was the edge of the one dark place remaining in Griff's memory—he couldn't recall any warning sound. Poole seemed to have appeared out of nowhere. Griff, at work below deck, had been unaware of Poole's presence until he had straightened up from the engine compartment. Then violence had followed swiftly—the rocking blow to Griff's head, the wrench falling, the spark, the blast propelling him like a circus performer shot out of a cannon. But Poole—— The deck had erupted directly under Poole's feet, and he had not come out of the water alive.

Griff brought himself to his feet, looking straight at Teague. The chief was playing cat-and-mouse with him. One question could prove it—a single, clear-cut, yes-or-no question which Teague could not evade.

"About Poole, whether or not he was in my boat when she blew up. What do you believe now? Was he aboard or wasn't he?"

Teague pursed his lips thoughtfully, looking down; and he shook his head. The chief hadn't put his lie into words, but it was still a lie.

"So he wasn't," Griff said stiffly. "And accidental death is no crime anyhow. Now I want to know where all this leaves me."

Teague hesitated, looking acutely embarrassed. Then, as if on cue, the door opened.

It was Dick Carrick who had his hand on the knob; he was smiling, courteously ushering Lynn into the room.

Griff felt a surge of gladness at seeing Lynn, and instant concern. The swelling on her jaw shocked him; the bruise was livid and ugly against her unnatural paleness. Her smile was hesitant, and her eyes—— Afraid? Griff couldn't understand why she should seem afraid of him.

"They wouldn't let me come sooner, Griff," Lynn said. "Are you all right?"

"That's okay," Griff said awkwardly. "I'm fine."

Carrick was all good cheer. "Thought I'd look in, Griff, just in case you needed a lawyer." He laughed casually, turning to Teague. "You aren't holding this man, are you?"

136

"What would I charge him with?" Teague said in a disgruntled tone. "No; he's free to go."

"Well, then!" Carrick chuckled at Griff. "What are you waiting for?"

Lynn said quietly. "I'll drive you home, Griff."

Teague unlocked the street door for them. Griff followed Lynn, grateful for the cooler air outside but feeling oddly uneasy. Looking back, he saw Carrick and Teague gazing after them both with a curiously self-satisfied look on their faces—two men, to judge from their expressions, who had put over a neat deal. Griff wondered. Carrick's entrance with Lynn, at just the right moment, might have been part of a staged scene.

Accompanying Lynn to her open convertible, Griff felt, too, a constraint in her—not shyness born of their estrangement, but a strange sort of cautiousness which she was trying to conceal. He closed the car door and stood there while she sat at the wheel, looking up at him, her nearness a reality so vivid he could not quite believe it.

"Dad said you wanted to see me, Griff."

"What I had to say—— I can't say it now." Griff tightened his hands on the edge of the door. "For one thing, I'm in trouble. I don't know much about it, except that it's bad. Lynn—— Does it have anything to do with you?"

Quickly she looked away. "What do you mean, Griff?"

"Does it?"

"Have anything to do with me? I want to help you if I can—in that way it does."

"I'll need help to get out of this all right," Griff said. "Dan didn't want to let me go just now. There's a gimmick in it somewhere. I think it's his way of giving me enough rope."

He saw an instant of consternation in Lynn's eyes.

"This is something I've got to get cleared up before I

can tell you what I had to say." Abruptly he straightened, pushing his fists deep into his pockets. "I thought, until now—Lynn, I've hoped you'd want to make a new try with me. I see now you don't. All right. That's that— you've made up your mind."

She was gazing at him in small panic of bewilderment.

"Thanks, but I don't need a ride," Griff said heavily. "I'll walk."

He turned away, conscious that Lynn was gazing after him. His need for her was so deep it was a sickness, but he did not look back. The dreadful sense of aloneness he had felt last night, foundering out there in the black bay, had returned to him. One glance had plunged him into it again—seeing that Lynn was no longer wearing her wedding-ring.

CHAPTER XIII

LYNN STOOD AT *Julie*'s wheel, holding her in an easterly course across Boca Palma Bay. It was afternoon again, a brilliant autumn day, the water satin-smooth. Because her father's cruiser was out of commission while a new engine was being installed, Lynn had asked Dick Carrick's permission to borrow his motor-boat for a few hours. Tim Hampden, hearing that she meant to run out to Pelican Key, had asked if he might come along; his old outboard runabout had been on the ways all this week, getting her hull scraped and painted, and he wanted to see Bill Rockwood on a matter of business. She had assented readily, of course, although she had come to feel uneasy with Tim; he could not hide his profound hurt and reproach, convinced as he was that her marriage to Griff had brought them both to tragic consequences.

Hampden sat withdrawn on the cockpit deck, watching Lynn in a mood of morose admiration while she handled *Julie* with a practised smoothness. She was wearing a strapless golden-yellow swim-suit and matching sandals of raffia. The sunshine on her bare shoulders and legs had a summery sting in it, and the breeze in her face was delightfully soft. In Tim Hampden, however, there was no enjoyment of the moment. She was conscious of his brooding gaze. Trying not to let it disturb her, she watched the busy bay—sailboats skimming, fishermen trolling, a family of porpoises rolling lazily. Suddenly she closed the throttle.

"There's Griff." She pointed off the starboard beam. "There in the white rowboat with the red kicker."

Griff's broad back was turned towards them, nut-brown against the white of his swimming-trunks. It was twenty-four hours since Lynn had last seen him. Having failed to reach him by phone earlier today, she had hoped to find him at his cottage on Pelican Key. Instead, here he was offshore, anchored in a boat that didn't belong to him—rented or borrowed. He was sitting with his shoulders bent, resting in an attitude of weary discouragement. As Lynn watched, he fitted a diver's mask over his face, then brought himself up, and in one easy curving motion dropped himself overboard with scarcely a splash.

"Remember what Dick and Spence told you about the way the ransom was picked up?" Hampden said caustically. "Slick and tricky, done by an expert swimmer."

It was almost like suspecting a man because he could walk—these warm waters attracted and encouraged swimmers by the thousands. Yet Lynn could not brush aside the fact that it was an added point against Griff.

"Is that the spot where *Lotus* went down, Tim?" Knowing how much that work-scarred old boat had meant to Griff, Lynn felt sorry for him. "Will he be able to salvage any of her?"

"Damned little. The engine maybe, the propeller, a few odds and ends." Hampden answered in a voice so cynical that Lynn turned quickly to look at him. "Don't let it fool you. This is a phony show of innocence. A few pieces of junk aren't of any importance to him—not when he has one hundred thousand Armstead dollars cached away somewhere."

Lynn turned forward without speaking again and eased the throttle open. This was not a good time to approach Griff. Hampden was impatient, and Lynn needed to talk with Griff in private—if he would talk with her at all. Looking back once, she saw that he had surfaced and was heaving something into the rowing-boat. Intent on his task, he had not noticed *Julie*.

They moored *Julie* to the pier in the cove. Following Hampden towards the fork in the path leading to Bill Rockwood's lonely house, Lynn gazed regretfully at the cypress cottage on the hummock where she and Griff had begun their marriage.

From the first Spencer Armstead had vehemently objected to it as a home for Lynn. "Shameful, my daughter living under such hardships!"—meaning the small inconveniences of island isolation which she hadn't really minded. Too late she had realized she never should have persuaded Griff to leave it in favour of a rented house in Belle Loma. Why had she yielded to her father? She had hoped it might help to win his support and friendship for her new husband. Instead it had opened the way to further interferences with their independence. To Griff it had seemed more and more that Spencer Armstead was ordering their lives, and soon the inevitable rebellion had widened the breach. Looking back on it now, Lynn could blame herself for a serious, irreversible mistake.

On the farther side of the island Bill Rockwood's home sat alone above a small crescent of beach, looking across water empty to the horizon. Although the grounds were meticulously kept, and walled against the encroachment of the jungle, it invariably seemed deserted—an odd impression, since its recluse owner hadn't left it for so long as one whole day in the more than thirty years since his grandiose venture had fallen in ruins. He had obdurately resolved then to stay put until eventually the time would come when fortune's forces would build it up again. The townspeople of Belle Loma had laughed at him behind his back for that, but it was a joke no longer. All of Florida was flourishing on an even grander scale than anyone had envisaged then.

Lynn supposed that Bill Rockwood, constantly alert for invasions of his privacy, had heard them approaching; he was probably at a window, or screening himself somewhere in the gardens, watching to see whether or not they were intruders to be summarily warned off. He hadn't yet appeared when they went through the gate.

Lynn stopped just inside, silently startled. The patio on this side of the house was paved with coquina shells, many-coloured and shaped like tiny butterflies, which were a by-product of Bill Rockwood's coquina broth, his favourite delicacy. Using a hand-made sieve of hardware cloth, he had collected all these countless millions of them, little by little, in the surf of the little beach below. Crunching underfoot, they gave off exactly the same sound Lynn had heard outside the kidnappers' hideaway that cold dawn when Griff had been there, walking about and unconsciously whistling.

Her thoughts took an alarmed leap to the old construction-gang shack back in the jungle. The trash heap behind it was used by both Griff and Bill. . . . Quickly she told herself that to suspect Bill Rockwood was unthinkable. As for this charming patio—— Many Florida home owners, avoiding the endless problem of keeping a lawn green under the intense summer sun, spread their yards with gravel or a mixture of crushed shells. Bill Rockwood's, except for his unique use of pure coquina, was not different from hundreds of others.

Tim Hampden was about to knock when the owner of the island opened the door. Bill Rockwood was a man who could outbrood Hampden—full-waisted, short, bald, he seemed at first glance to be a jolly sort—Lynn could recall how, as a little girl, she had delighted in his ebullient good nature—but years of self-imposed solitude had drained and dried it out of him and he had become habitually solemn-faced. He hadn't, however, forgotten entirely what a smile was—after an expressionless glance at Hampden he summoned up a small one for Lynn—small but warmly sincere.

He greeted them with grave cordiality, asked Lynn about Griff, and invited them inside. The living-room sprawled. The walls were time-darkened pecky cypress, the beams hand-hewn oak. A series of broad picture-windows invited philosophical contemplation of all creation. It was a place of masculine creature comforts, including the oak-panelled bar at one side, where favoured guests had carved their names. While Bill Rockwood mixed drinks for them there, making an intensely serious and personal operation of it, Lynn glanced around, disquieted by returning misgivings.

Bill Rockwood had built this gracious house of eight large rooms at a time of expansive hope. Several years later his wife had died. His two sons had gone directly from college into engineering and had soon married. Living alone here, he had no use for all its space. The north wing had been closed off for many years. *"The hide-out—on or near the water—closed for a long time. The floor—loose sand on it"*—or possibly an accumulation of gritty dust? *"A characteristic smell. . . ."* Finding herself drawing air heedfully into her nostrils, Lynn shook her head, ashamed of her doubts.

Rockwood brought them their drinks, a rum concoction of his own invention—a Pelican Swizzle, he called it, and the secret of its ingredients, as so much of his later life had been, was his alone. He sat, sipped gently, and tongued the cold dew off his upper lip, enjoying the mystery of it as much as the flavour. All this was something of a ceremony, a prelude to conversation.

"It's been a long time," he began, now that his guests were settled comfortably with their tall, ice-packed glasses. "Something on your minds. Both of you."

"You know why I'm here," Hampden said in his matter-of-fact manner. "Time's running short. I ought to have a decision, or at least some indication to work on."

The taste of nectar in Bill Rockwood's mouth turned sour. "Griff's option has two more weeks to run. Until then I'll hold to it. I'll give him until the last minute."

"But will he pick it up? Can he? And if not? I can't very well wait until the last minute to know what then."

Rockwood let Hampden's impatient questions hang in the air and turned his gaze fondly on Lynn. "I'd sign a renewal if I could. Sign it without another penny from Griff. But——" He rubbed one hand over his bald head as if it ached from too much thinking. "I'm an old man, honey. I haven't much time left for more dreaming. Fact is, I've given it up—at long last I've come to know I'll never see this island as Griff's father and I longed to see it. Besides, my money's finally running out. It lasted more than thirty years but now it's almost gone. I'll have to sell."

Hampden grasped at that. "Well, this is more like it! If I can depend——"

"But I still won't commit myself," Rockwood broke in, "until Griff's last chance is gone. Think me a sentimental old mule if you like. I always wanted Griff to carry on for his dad and me. After he married Lynn I wanted it even more, for both of them. I still do."

Lynn thought how strange it was that this man could hold a deep and lasting affection for her while remaining for decades implacably hostile to her father. She had never known the reason in detail. It went back to her childhood, when the development of Pelican Key was a booming promise. At its earliest stages, a time of phrenetic speculation, Lynn's father had undertaken, through some sort of financial manipulation, to undercut the Rockwood–Griffth project. The attempt to wrest the island from the partners had failed, but only after a bitter controversy, and since then the mutual enmity between Spencer Armstead and Bill Rockwood had never lost its edge.

"As long as Griff's option holds," Rockwood repeated firmly, "I'll not consider other proposals."

"Suppose, in some way, he does manage to exercise it." Hampden glanced significantly at Lynn. "He'll be stymied at the start. He won't be able to swing the rest without heavy backing and he can't get that. He's already tried and failed over and over. Investors with that kind of money won't risk——"

"I know what such investors have told Griff," Rockwood broke in quietly. "He's too young, he lacks experience, he's too small an operator. The essential problems are too big for him, too much for a small isolated community to handle—fresh water, electric power, sewers, police, and fire protection. Pelican Key is too far out—a bridge connecting with the mainland would be too costly and involve too many questions of easements. Nobody but boat owners could live here, and they would live under constant threat of the weather—one bad hurricane could wipe the entire investment out of existence."

Rockwood sipped his drink again. "None of these reasons is valid. Fresh water? This island was a water stop for the Spanish galleons; the old well is still here. Until a bridge is built a ferry will do. There will be a bridge some day, not a single long span, but a series of causeways from key to key. Other islands have solved the same civic problems, and all of them will be solved here." To Bill Rockwood, a man of enduring faith, the matter was not arguable.

"The whole trouble is that the financiers see *too* good a thing here. They're greedy—they want full control, which Griff won't give them. He's in their way, this small-fry dreamer; they want to be rid of him. Let them have their own plans, their own contractors, their own engineers, then they'll pour their money in eagerly enough, and before long the profits will pour back into their own pockets." Rockwood leaned towards Hampden, his face hardened. "Of course that's the whole purpose of this syndicate you're representing."

Lynn sat up. This was unsettling news. "What syndicate?"

"They call themselves Boca Palma Associates," Rockwood answered. "Who are they? I don't know—although your friend Hampden, here, is probably one of them."

Hampden protested flatly. "No. I'm acting as their agent and I'll be paid an agent's standard fee, that's all. I'm not in the deal itself."

"Who are they, then?" Rockwood asked again, this time directly of Hampden.

"I'm bound not to tell you. For good, solid reasons of business I can't——"

"Griff went to your office and asked you the same question, wanting to know who he's up against. A fair question. You two had a hot set-to about it. He came away not knowing any more than you'd already told me, which is next to nothing. Damned strange that a man can't find out who's bucking him."

"There's nothing unusual about it, Bill. It's essential to any big, new enterprise in its formative stage. I'm simply acting under the instructions of the Associates' attorney, Dick Carrick."

"Ah? Carrick's one who's in it, is he?"

"Whether Dick is putting any money of his own into it, I can't say. My dealings are with the Associates' front man. I've already told you who he is—Ken Simpson, at the bank. Ken's acting not as a banker, but as a private investor. That's all I can tell you."

"Why are they hiding behind an organization with a fancy name? Why aren't they willing to do business in the open?"

"Bill, this is accepted practice, and you know the reasons for it as well as I do. We don't want values to be inflated out of sight overnight. We want to keep unscrupulous speculators and political opportunists away from it. A bonafide corporation wants to operate in good faith. A project of this size is always handled as quietly as possible until the basic contracts are all set."

"I have ways of finding out for myself," Bill Rockwood said steadily. "I might have a good idea right now who some of them are."

"Damn it all, Bill, nobody's trying to put anything over on you!"

"But you're asking me to sell my island to a bunch of men who aren't willing to show me their faces."

Hampden's face grew hot. He stood. "Let's not lose our tempers over it, Bill. You've had their offer. It stands as long as Griff's option is in force. I've been instructed to say this to you—after that their figure may drop sharply. It's a fair bargain and I feel you ought to accept it. Meanwhile you have time to think it over." He added, "Thanks for the drink," and turned to Lynn. "I'll wait for you on the pier."

He left the room quickly, still controlling his exasperation. Lynn found Bill Rockwood's gaze on her, commiserating with her.

"I'm sorry, honey, hellish sorry it's put Griff in such a bad spot—but one way or the other I'll have to sell."

She asked carefully, "Does Griff know that?"

"Last time we talked it over, a week ago, I had to tell him. Once his option expires, he'll lose it forever—all this." Rockwood wagged his head ruefully, then managed another small smile. "But he's still trying, and I want to think he'll make it somehow."

Lynn studied Rockwood's face in troubled indecision. Without realizing it, he had underscored the motive which her father had imputed to Griff. Or—was he cleverly covering for Griff—preparing her for a last-minute coup? It hardly mattered which was true—both implied guilt, and the second, confirming the first, implied further that Rockwood knew what Griff had done. Lynn could not go so far as to believe Rockwood had been Griff's accomplice —that would be evil twice compounded, too dreadful to believe—but in some way had he learned——? Was he actually covering for Griff?

Her quick impulse was to attack the possibility, to demolish it if possible. "Bill—— You've heard about Alec Poole. Did you know him?"

"Poole?" Rockwood nodded slowly. "I let him fish in the cove when he wanted to. Sometimes he tied up there for the night. Came in once or twice to drink and talk. Odd sort, you had to watch him, but good company. I rather liked him."

"Did Griff know him?"

"Imagine so. Couldn't help running into each other here and there, could they?"

"But—didn't you ever see them talking together—talking something over?"

Rockwood frowned at her curiously and shook his head.

"Have you any idea why Alec Poole was in Griff's boat when she blew up?"

"Well!" Rockwood lifted his eyebrows. "Was he?"

Lynn found herself standing, suddenly and frantically needing to get away from this man and out of this house. She went quickly to the door. There she stopped, turned, and saw that Rockwood was following her with a look of uneasy astonishment in his eyes.

"Bill—— You *are* my friend?"

"The best, honey. Griff's too. Listen to me, Lynn. Griff's impulsive, sometimes hot-headed—and everybody makes mistakes, sometimes very bad ones. I know, I've lived with a great big one for thirty years. But you and Griff—so young, with so much ahead of you—yours can be unmade. There's nothing I want more than to see you and Griff back together."

It was at once a heart-warming and a monstrous thought—that this man should wish to see her reunited with a husband whom he secretly knew to be a criminal. Even a rich old friendship could be a pointing finger!

She could not go. A final question forced itself out.

"When Griff learned that you can't hang on any longer, that you're forced to sell now, to the syndicate if not to him—what did he do, what did he say?"

Bill Rockwood hesitated over his answer with a sombre frown. "Well—— I'm afraid it threw him into a state, Lynn. Never saw him so steamed up. A man who's held on to a dream as long and as hard as Griff has suddenly seeing he'll have to let it go, he can get pretty des——" Rockwood checked himself, shaking his head. "But that was a little while ago. A bad jolt, but he's had time to adjust to it. It'll work out, honey—if you'll help him.

Give him all the help he needs from you and it'll be all right."

Outside the house, Lynn still heard the thunder of the word Bill Rockwood had not spoken. *Desperate*, he had almost said. *Desperate*.

CHAPTER XIV

HAZY-GREEN AND SILENT, the water had taken on a chill. This would be Griff's last dive. Low over the rippled sandy bottom of the bay, his lungs beginning to burn, he kicked himself along.

He was about to go up when he saw it—another fire extinguisher lying half buried. He missed once before hooking his fingers on its handle. When he surfaced he swung it into the rowing-boat, tore off his mask, and hung in the water for a minute, breathing deeply. When he felt equal to another effort he hoisted himself aboard, pulled the flippers off his feet, and lay back in the warm sun.

Rested, he hauled in the anchor and started the outboard. While heading for Pelican Key he looked over the few pieces of gear which he had been able to bring up single-handed. The only undamaged articles, still useful, were three other fire extinguishers, one a gallon foamer, the others CO_2 guns. The fourth, the last one he had found, was a carbon tet type, the brand name Protecto. Griff examined it curiously. It didn't belong to him; he had had no such extinguisher aboard *Lotus*. He couldn't guess how it had happened to be lying near the sunken wreckage except through coincidence—evidently it had been lost overboard recently from some other boat.

He dismissed it as he veered towards the pier in the cove,

noticing *Julie* tied up there and Tim Hampden waiting. Hampden stood still, watching without a greeting, while Griff swung close. Griff dropped a clove hitch around a piling, puzzled by Hampden's fixed cold gaze. Surely, Griff thought, he wasn't remembering his broken engagement to Lynn—that old resentment couldn't account for it.

"Sorry about Hal," Griff said. "How is he?"

Quick rage coloured Hampden's face. He turned his back and walked away along the pier. Griff stared after him and saw Lynn hurrying down the path to meet him. So they had come here together. Lynn and Tim—had they turned back to each other? Griff steadied himself, feeling a new stab of despair.

He sat in the rowing-boat, absently examining the odd extinguisher, feeling the fluid sloshing inside it. Some of the stuff had been pumped out; it seemed to be only half full. When Lynn paused on the pier above him, Hampden at her side, he glanced up long enough to say hello, placed the extinguisher aside, and concentrated on the important business of putting on a shirt and a pair of old beat-up moccasins. The swim-suit Lynn was wearing was his favourite; she was all gold and soft brown, so pretty it hurt him to look at her.

"What are you going to do about getting a new boat, Griff?"

"I'll make out somehow."

Before she could speak again Hampden said shortly, "It's pretty late, Lynn, so let's get going."

"You take *Julie* then," she suggested. "I'll go back with Griff. That is, if Griff doesn't mind."

He shook his head. "Okay. Sure."

She sat on the edge of the pier, swinging her legs while Hampden cast off. *Julie* churned away and the quiet left in the cove became a shared intimacy.

Griff sat there feeling miserable to his marrow. Now

that he knew where he had been so wrong, and how he might have kept it right, it was too late. The conflicts of pride that had seemed so important then seemed incredibly trivial now—now that they had done their harm. Like that big convertible Lynn had bought just before their wedding because she'd known they wouldn't be able to afford anything like it afterwards. How she'd stocked up on expensive clothes. How she would suggest having dinner out—"I'll treat", then, driving her car, she would take him to a plushy restaurant where he felt out of place and uncomfortable in his cheap suit. How her gifts to him, on their birthdays and anniversary, outclassed his to her. And Spencer Armstead's—so ostentatiously generous that they seemed to be charity. The way he used to come from work in his rusty truck, wearing mud-caked hip boots, dirty as a tramp and smelling of muck, and Lynn so clean and pretty he couldn't touch her. She would tidy up after him—an abomination in his own home, and soap and water couldn't wash that feeling of inferiority out of him, or fresh clothes cover it. Little splinters festering, intensifying the deeper hurt of frustrations born of his own misjudgment. To Griff the successful development of Pelican Key would have been the fulfilment he had yearned to bestow on Lynn. As it was, she might as well have thrown herself away on any damn penniless clam-digger.

Then, when he was at his lowest ebb, his work constricted by a lack of new equipment, the Pelican Key project blocked, Lynn, with the best of intentions, had made a fatal move—she had offered to tear up their premarital property agreement. With that, Griff had felt, his wife had acknowledged him a visionary incapable of making a go of it on his own. He realized now, too late, that Lynn had instead meant it as an expression of faith in him; yet he could not have accepted it without confirming every malicious rumour that he had married her for her money, and her father's contemptuous estimate of him. It had created an intolerable impasse, and the strain to escape it had torn the bonds between them.

Lynn was speaking. Lost, Griff had scarcely heard her. He lifted his head.

"I said, I'm ready to hear what you have to tell me, Griff. Dad said it seemed urgent when you came to the house the other night, it was so late. Past midnight, wasn't it?"

There was something odd, Griff felt, in the way she had asked the question, but he couldn't put his finger on it.

"I didn't expect to find your dad still up. He usually goes to bed earlier than that. You often like to read fairly late. I thought I'd find you downstairs with a book. Just like me to bust in at the wrong time." He looked again at her left hand, at the pale circle left by her wedding-ring. "When are you going ahead with the divorce?"

"Do you still want it, Griff?"

His yearning for her overflowed his defences. "That's what I wanted to talk to you about. I've had a tough time getting to the point of admitting it, but I'd come to see how everybody else was right and I was crazy—in too deep, over my head. I'd decided to follow all the advice I've had about this island and forget it. It's been nothing but grief—it helped to split us up and it wasn't worth that. I thought if I went back to my old job and saved some money, and then started my own business again along the right track, and gradually built it up—well, you and I might——" He broke off. "What's the matter? You're looking at me as if——"

"Griff! You don't want Pelican Key any more? Do you really mean that?"

"It's what I'd made up my mind to tell you. I couldn't

wait. Then, when I couldn't see you right away—— Your dad said you were visiting the Courtenays, so I tried to reach you there. But——"

"Tried? How?"

That strange note in Lynn's voice again—it puzzled Griff. "Why, by phone. The last time we saw the Courtenays they were trying to get a phone. I thought maybe the line was put in by now. So I asked the Palmport operator to check. But she said no—they weren't listed."

"Griff! When was this?"

He couldn't imagine why she was practically screeching at him. "That same night. As soon as I got home."

"But what time was that, Griff? *What time?*"

"It was—— As near as I can remember—— About a quarter after one."

The expression that crossed Lynn's face then was even stranger—a look of heartfelt relief quickly followed by a pinch of doubt—and it was the doubt that stayed. He didn't understand it.

"What's so bothersome about that, Lynn?"

She didn't answer. First, for some baffling reason, she couldn't; then, when she seemed about to speak, they were interrupted by a familiar voice calling. Bill Rockwood was coming down the path.

"Griff——" Now Lynn abruptly changed the subject. "How well did you know Alec Poole?"

He held his head. "Poole, Poole! Why is that guy haunting me? Dan's out of his mind if he thinks I was mixed up in some kind of crooked deal with Poole."

"But you did know him, Griff. You were seen talking together more than once. What was it about?"

"Nothing," Griff groaned. "He'd come wandering around, here in the cove, or where I was working on a job. Once he turned up on my pier. Always killing time. Talk together? Sure we did—small talk and not much of that.

153

I was too busy. Until Dan started grilling me about him I wasn't even sure of his name."

Lynn was uncertainly silent; and Griff was thinking.

"One thing about him—he seemed interested in my boat in some special way. But maybe I was mistaken about that. Maybe he was just trying to get loose from that dizzy girl of his for a few minutes. He kept ordering her to stop tagging after him. She was always yakking questions at him, driving him nuts. If he scratched his nose she wanted to know why, and if he told her it itched she wouldn't believe him. She must have had good reason not to trust him about anything. I wouldn't have either, not a dime's worth, not a shifty character like Poole."

"But Griff, listen! Didn't you ever talk to him about your plans for this island—your option?"

He frowned at her. "Why should I?"

Lynn was shaking her head in confusion when Bill Rockwood stopped at her side.

"Well, boy," Rockwood said, soberly hearty, "you're in pretty fine shape for a guy who might have been blown to bits. I went over to the police office as soon as I found out it was your boat, but I couldn't get past Dan Teague. Close-mouthed cop, not giving out any information at all. Why wasn't he letting anybody get near you?"

"I don't know," Griff said. "He suspects me of something serious, but I can't even figure what it is."

"Wanted to tell you," Bill Rockwood went on, "—something peculiar happened right after the explosion. I heard it, of course—hustled right down to this pier and put out fast. Heard a boat tearing away. Couldn't see it—no lights. Sure as hell it was somebody who didn't want to be seen around there. It was scooting along the shore, keeping close, then out, circling towards——"

"What?" Griff was staring at him. "Say that again!"

"I said that right after the explosion some other boat

154

headed away from there at top speed, with no running lights, and swung over towards the north of Belle Loma."

It was Rockwood's turn, and Lynn's to stare. Griff's face was like a light, shining with a burst of realization.

This was what he had been trying to draw out of the last dark crypt of his memory. This was what had left him with such a nightmarish feeling of abandonment while he was struggling half-consciously to keep afloat. He recalled it now—a lightless boat speeding, not towards him, but away, farther and farther away. And the dead body of Alec Poole wallowing in the black bay behind it.

"Griff!" Lynn blurted. "I'm coming with you!"

She dropped into the boat as he cast off. At the first snap of the pull rope the outboard howled into action. Griff remembered to wag a so-long to Rockwood. Lynn braced herself, the wind rippling in her hair. She screeched a question at Griff, but the exhaust was too loud; he shook his head and kept the throttle wide open, his eyes alive with anticipation. Beyond the cove he veered the boat into the channel; then he swung it again, sharply towards Belle Loma, and headed straight for the pier of the Azalea Motel.

Alec Poole's cabin cruiser was still tied up there. Cutting the power, Griff eased close beside her. He threw a line across, rapidly made it fast, and took up the Protecto fire extinguisher. He jumped aboard *Playgirl* and caught Lynn's hand, steadying her as she followed.

He hadn't far to look. There on the starboard side of the cockpit was an empty metal clip. The Protecto fitted into it easily, perfectly.

On the port side Griff found a second clip holding another extinguisher in place—another Protecto, a duplicate of the one he had found on the bottom of the bay.

"What does it mean, Griff?"

"When," Griff said, his eyes wide on Lynn. "That's the big question—when did he lose it?"

She ran along the pier after him and past the parked cars until they reached the little office fronting on Gulf Boulevard. The motel owner was sitting at his desk, reading a newspaper. He looked up in astonishment at this hasty young man and this breathless girl.

"Mr. Clane—— You know about my boat, how it blew up night before last. Now about Alec Poole—— Was he out on the bay near there when it happened?"

Mr. Clane had to take time to think about it. "Why, Griff, I don't rightly know *where* he was. Big bay, you know, runs miles to the north and 'way over to Palmport Point and on down——"

"But was he out?" Griff insisted.

Mr. Clane thought again. "Well, I didn't see him putting out, Griff. Can't say I did. Hadn't paid any attention. He came and went at all odd hours, you know. Can't say either whether his boat was at the pier at the time—I mean when I heard that loud bang out on the water. But—— You know, it was a funny thing——"

Griff forced himself to wait, afire with impatience, Lynn's cautioning hand on his arm.

"Noticed something a little later," Mr. Clane went on slowly. "Thought it was peculiar because other boats around here were all heading out to see what'd happened. That's when I heard a boat putting in. Made me sort of curious, so I stepped outside for a look. Didn't see any boat heading inshore—but Mr. Poole's boat was back there then."

Poole himself had not been running *Playgirl*. At that moment Poole was afloat in the bay, his dead body to be found within a few minutes.

"Poole's boat came in right after the explosion?" Griff asked carefully.

"Well, now, I didn't actually see her coming in. When I looked she was already tied up. Of course, somebody could've made a quick job of it. I figured she must've been brought in just a minute before, because somebody was there on the pier——"

"Somebody?"

"A man."

"A man who'd just docked Poole's boat! Mr. Clane—— Who was it?"

"Pretty dark, you know. He wasn't holding still either. Instead of watching what was going on out there on the bay, he took off, running. Didn't come past the south side of the building, here where the lights are, but dodged along the back like he didn't want anybody to see him."

"But you did get a look at him?"

"In a way I did. I mean I saw him hustling off along the road. He might have had a car parked up there somewhere. Got that impression. Didn't try to follow him, of course—just watched him for a minute until he was out of sight. Bushes along the road up there, you know, other cars parked, and he got off behind them, still hustling. Wondered why he was in such a big hurry."

Lynn asked quickly, "Didn't you see who he was, Mr. Clane?"

"No," Mr. Clane said. "No, I wouldn't have the faintest idea who he might've been."

Griff had one more question. A desperately hopeful question: "Was that man *carrying* anything?"

Mr. Clane looked astonished. "Now, that's another funny thing. If you hadn't asked me, I wouldn't've thought of it. Yes, Yes, he was."

"Carrying *what*?"

"Couldn't be entirely sure of that. Might've been a box." Mr. Clane made motions with his hands, indicating size. "About so, square and flat. . . . Say, you seem pretty worked up, you two. Is this sort of special to you in some way?"

Mr. Clane went unanswered. Griff and Lynn were gazing out of the window and along the highway. It was straight and busy and colourful in the bright sunlight. They were picturing it in darkness, watching a shadow fleeing along the sandy shoulder—the shadow of an unknown man.

CHAPTER XV

THEY WERE BACK inside that hotbox of a first-aid room.

After tying the borrowed rowing-boat to the municipal pier, Griff and Lynn had come straight to Dan Teague's desk—Griff carrying the Protecto fire extinguisher. He had barely started talking when the chief had cut him off. It was time for the early night shift to take over, and patrolmen were wandering in and out of the front office at odd moments. It hadn't mattered to Griff that they might overhear him, but somehow it had mattered to Teague. He had hurriedly brought them in here and closed the door.

"Why make a hush-hush thing of this?" Griff asked. "You don't want your men to know you're capable of making big mistakes—is that it?"

Teague's face paled with resentment. Lynn, sitting on the cot, warned him with her eyes. She was right; this was a bad beginning; but he was too sore to be careful.

"Mistakes?" Teague said, biting it off.

"Two. First, turning me loose. You thought I'd make a slip, I'd trip myself up, but I've come back with something important, something you should have found for ourself. You didn't think to ask Mr. Clane a few simple questions about Alec Poole's boat."

"I'm always eager to learn," Teague said in an abrasive voice. "Go on, tell me how to run my office."

"That's another thing—I've got a feeling you're not running it. You're not your own man any more. Somebody wants me to be guilty—of what I don't know, but anyhow guilty. You're under pressure from the outside and playing along. You seem to need a scapegoat, and I'm it. What kind of chief are you?—not wanting anybody to hear any evidence in a suspected man's favour!"

"Watch it, Griff!" Teague held himself taut. "I'll admit this much. One crook put a fast one over on me and got away—Poole. It won't happen again. I've promised myself to nail Poole's accomplice, no matter who he is, regardless of anybody's influence. If that sounds too damn noble for your taste, you don't know me."

"Then listen to what I'm trying to tell you. It's about Poole's accomplice. Poole and some other man had been far across the bay in that boat. It was the other man who brought it back, leaving Poole dead in the water. He——"

"Did Clane actually see him bringing it in?"

The question stopped Griff. The answer came hard. "No."

"So Clane simply saw it tied up there where it belonged. He can't say how long it had been there. He saw a man on the pier. The man hurried away. This is supposed to prove some point or other, I'm not sure what. You'd better start a little farther back. Let's hear this latest version of yours from the beginning."

Griff dropped the extinguisher on the cot beside Lynn, giving her a disheartened look. Teague, despite his training and experience, was displaying an all-too-human weakness. He was furious with himself because Poole had tricked him, and he had vented his resentment of Poole on

Griff. Now, when he sorely needed to vindicate himself Griff was telling him he had bungled again. His rankling sense of shame wouldn't allow him to admit it. He would never accept Griff's story without resisting it to the last detail.

"I was used," Griff said, accepting that challenge quietly. "That's the whole thing—I was used."

"By Poole?"

"By Poole and this other man, both of them working together. The other man kept himself under cover while Poole nosed around. He'd been watching how I came and went across the bay. He was curious about my boat. Looking back now, I can see he was planning some sort of tricky move, something he didn't want me to know about, or that red-headed babe of his either."

"First you said you weren't even slightly acquainted with Poole," Teague reminded him. "Suddenly you know all about him, what he was doing, even what he was thinking. Well, you have the advantage there. At least Poole can't contradict you."

"It stands to reason, Dan, judging from what happened Poole and his crooked pal had some hot money in their possession. You mentioned a robbery somewhere. Was that it? Bank-loot being smuggled into Belle Loma? Whatever it was, you knew it was on its way, you were waiting for some signal or other to tell you——"

"I'm not giving out information," Teague said, eyeing Griff. "I'm getting educated."

"Once Poole and his side-kick had it, they hid it on *Lotus*——"

Teague cut in. "Why? With a hundred other boats to choose from, why pick yours?"

Griff felt sure the chief knew the answer as well as he did; but he spelled it out. He recalled the tension here in the police office the other night. Teague had been on duty unusually late, sleepless, waiting for something to break. And it had broken. All the signs said so—the helicopter scouting about before dawn, the Coast Guard's day-long rush of boat inspections. Something had triggered all this, and Poole must have expected it and guarded himself against it.

"You mean he had an inside tip?" Teague asked evenly.

"Looks like it. That's a question to dig into. If so, where did the tip come from?"

Teague set his mouth and said nothing. Griff went on doggedly. Poole and his accomplice must have been short of time. Certainly they had been anxious to avoid making a suspicious move. They couldn't risk being seen together. Above all, they couldn't run the chance of getting caught with the money red-handed. What could they do? Expecting, as they had, a flurry of police action, how could they play it safe?

These two men, Griff said, had seen that they must lie low for twenty-four hours or longer, until the worst of the heat was off; but first they must get their loot cached away in a hurry, and quietly. The essential thing had been to stow it in an unlikely place which would be close at hand, yet dissociated from them, and safe—one which they could watch from a near distance without arousing suspicion; and later they must somehow get it beyond the reach of the searchers without being spotted. They had solved these problems and avoided these risks by making secret use of Griff's boat.

A smart choice, Griff pointed out. He was the only boatman in town who shuttled over to Pelican Key, the farthermost island in the bay, regularly and often. The money hidden on *Lotus* would be more secure than it would have been anywhere else, simply because Griff was a long-time member of the Auxiliary and the Coast Guard would pass his boat without a look. Poole and his accomplice would simply sit back confidently and wait until Griff, all unawares, had carried the money well outside the area of danger.

"Poole must have sneaked aboard *Lotus* during the previous night while she was moored at my pier. I was away from home for hours that night, restless, fighting out a big decision with myself. I went to Lynn's father's place, then stopped in here, and when I hit the sack it was about one-thirty. If Poole hadn't already done the job by then, he must have slipped in after I was asleep. I didn't hear any noises. He must have been careful about using a light. His pal may have stood watch while he crowded himself down in the engine compartment and went to work. Squirming around, he unintentionally bent the fuel line and started a slow leak, and being in a hurry he didn't notice it. Except for that leak I wouldn't have found the money—it would have stayed there until they were ready to sneak it out again."

"You're turning handsprings," Teague said. "Before, you denied knowing anything about that package of money. Now you admit it was hidden in your boat."

"Not one package." Griff was giving it to Teague squarely, unafraid of his facts. "*Two* packages."

"Ah? It's all straightened out in your mind now, is it? Two packages! Then what became of the second package, the one I didn't find in the bay? Can you explain all about that too?"

"I'm coming to it. Those two men knew that four or five times a week I spend the night at the cottage on Pelican Key. They expected me to run across the next evening, so they went over in Poole's boat, anchored somewhere offshore near the cove, and waited for me to show. They had it all prearranged. When the way was clear they'd come in, get the money out of *Lotus*, then take it on to some new hiding-place out there, or maybe two separate hiding-places, where they could leave it indefinitely. **But it** didn't work out like that.

"Watching me, they saw me haul up short of the cove. That must have puzzled them because they didn't know about the fuel leak. Then, when they saw me going below, into the engine compartment, it must have scared them plenty. What if I found the hidden money? They'd lose it—I'd probably take it straight back here to the police office, unless they got it away from me first. That involved a new risk, exposing themselves to me, but they had no choice. So Poole headed his boat towards mine——"

"I remember now——"

"Ah-h?"

"—hearing a boat close by. I was below, hunting for the leak, so I wasn't sure and I was too busy to look. By that time Poole had cut his engine. He drifted close, came aboard without making any noise, and caught me unawares. I'd already found the packages and put one on the deck. He grabbed it up and tossed it to the other man in the boat alongside. Then, when I straightened, he slugged me, intending to get away with the second package too. But that idea didn't work out either. The explosion blew it to bits."

"You remember it all now, all of it so damned clearly. Amazing." Teague's voice was acrid. "Well, go on. What comes next?"

Griff shook his head. "It's nothing I can remember, because I didn't see it. The rest is partly a guess, but I think it's in the groove. I was blown clear, and something of the same sort must have happened to Poole. The explosion may have killed him, but I doubt that, because you said his head——"

Lynn put in, "That's right, Griff. Both his legs were broken, but the real reason he died——"

"His head beaten in, Dan said." Lynn nodded and

Griff went on rapidly, ignoring Teague's stormy scowl. "That's it then. Look at it from the viewpoint of the man in Poole's boat. There was Poole in the water, maybe knocked cold, maybe scarcely conscious. The other man was in a really big panic now—he had to get away from there fast. He could abandon Poole, but if he did Poole might come out of it alive and talk. If he pulled Poole aboard there would be endless questions, real trouble. Either way Poole spelled disaster for him, and there was only one way out. He grabbed a fire extinguisher, hit Poole over the head with it, killed him—then got away under full power, without lights. Taking that one package of money along, and nobody to divide it with now."

Griff saw a glitter in Teague's eyes, but it was unreadable.

"I heard that boat heading away. So did Bill Rockwood hear it."

Teague shrugged. "Could have been somebody with an illegal catch of fish wanting to avoid arrest."

"Mr. Clane heard it pulling into the motel pier."

"Nothing to show it was the same boat."

"But Mr. Clane saw somebody running off the pier, then along the road with the package under one arm. That's your man, Dan!"

"A mysterious man, disappearing into nowhere. No description, nothing. How do I go about finding him? Any suggestions?"

Griff couldn't answer.

"Clane's story is pretty damn vague, but I'll check it. As a matter of routine. In an effort to make up for past mistakes." Teague had a cold question. "That fire extinguisher belongs on Poole's boat, does it? Where'd you get hold of it?"

"Found it on the bottom of the bay. The man who hit Poole must have dropped it overboard after——"

164

"Got a witness? Somebody who actually saw you pull that thing out of the water at that spot? Did Lynn?"

"No." Griff's face turned icy. "You still don't believe me. My word isn't any good here."

"Not without corroboration."

With that Griff gave it up. The wall of doubt that Teague had built between them was impenetrable. In Lynn's face he saw compassion clouded over by hurt bewilderment. It was beyond his understanding. In some incomprehensible way they had been touched deep by evil; it had poisoned them all. . . . Griff turned to the door and paused; on hopelessness.

Lynn had checked her impulse to go with Griff because she felt a need to talk with Dan Teague. He gave her no opening. As the latch clicked he purposefully took her arm; he steered her out the street door and to his official car. They started north along Belle Loma Way.

"Dan, what am I to think? I know how strong the evidence is against Griff." She knew it even better than the chief—Griff's whistling outside the hide-out and Vina's point-blank accusation, neither of which she had told anyone. "But listening to him talk—Dan, he doesn't even know what happened to me."

"A couple of extra-smart planners pulled that job," Teague said, driving steadily at the speed limit, "and Poole wasn't the brain in it either. To a mind like that, slick lying comes easy."

"But Griff has explained several things without my even asking him about them. The phone call is one—the call that was recorded at one-thirteen the morning they brought me back. He simply mentioned that he'd tried to reach me at the Courtenays."

"At that exact same minute?" Teague smiled sceptically. "Remember what Dick Carrick said—it couldn't be a coincidence. The chances are millions to one against it."

Lynn wavered again, unable to argue the point. "But the fire extinguisher too. Poole *was* killed, wasn't he, by being struck on the head?"

"That threw me for a few seconds," Teague admitted. "Doc Elder had it right—two powerful blows with something cylindrical in shape. The extinguisher·fills the bill perfectly."

"Then how can you doubt——?"

"Crooks fall out. They double-cross each other. A pile of money was at stake. There's nothing to show it wasn't Griff himself who swung that extinguisher on Poole. He's trying to fast-talk himself out of it by accusing a ghost."

Lynn was silent as the chief turned the car into the courtyard of the Azalea Motel. He braked with an angry thrust at the pedal.

"Lynn, I'll lay it on the line with you. My part in this makes me sick, but what else can I do? I'm not being too tough on Griff. Actually he's getting every break. He can thank your father for that—the way your father insists on keeping it hushed up as much as possible, mostly for your sake. Otherwise Griff would be locked up right now, and charged, and facing a damned sure conviction. Everything's against him, every damned thing. Yet—— Show me one fact, just one good solid piece of evidence to prove Griff is innocent, and I'll be only too glad to make the most of it."

"It's right here, Dan," Lynn said confidently. "Mr. Clane did see a man dodging away from Alec Poole's boat with a package of ransom money."

Teague didn't answer. They turned to the motel office together. The owner was still seated at his desk, still rereading the same newspaper. He looked up curiously and volunteered an item of information.

"Something to ask you. Miss Daly, she's checking out

in the morning. Taking the body up to Virginia for burial. She's paying all the expenses, of course—Mr. Poole was broke. Any objection to her leaving?"

Teague shook his head. "This person you told Griff and Lynn about, the one who ran off your pier right after the explosion, and up the road. You sure it was a man?"

"Certainly wasn't a woman," Mr. Clane said.

"But couldn't it have been a teen-ager, say a boy big for his age?"

Mr. Clane turned it over in his mind. "Could've been. Plenty of 'em running loose."

"We have a lot of trouble with juveniles here. They prowl and steal, some of them—hub caps, radiator ornaments, anything they can get loose."

"I know that. Sometimes they start spooking around here, those crazy delinquents. Then I keep a sharp eye on my guests' cars."

"Now this boy or man went hustling away with a square, flat article, something he may have stolen from Poole's boat. Could it have been an ordinary buoyant cushion?"

Mr. Clane looked astonished. "Why, now, never thought of that. Since you mention it, that's exactly what it looked like. Why, sure, that's just what it was—one of those kapok cushions."

"Thanks, Mr. Clane," Teague said grimly.

His hand on Lynn's arm brought her outside the office. Verging on tears, she stood looking up into the set face of this officer who had so easily trumped Griff's only ace.

"Give me one good solid fact in Griff's favour," Teague said again. "Just one."

CHAPTER XVI

Teague stopped the sedan in the driveway of the Armstead home. Lynn, miserably at loose ends, had kept her troubled thoughts to herself since leaving the motel. She opened the car door, swung her legs out, then paused, turning an appealing look out on the chief.

"Dan, if we could find the hide-out mightn't that help?"

"Big job," Teague said without enthusiasm. "Plenty of territory to cover all around the bay, most of it outside my bailiwick. Help Griff? How? What would it prove either way?"

"It might turn out to be a place associated with someone other than Griff."

"Or it might not. Why spend time hunting for it when we've already got our man?" Teague turned tired eyes on her. "Lynn, a friendly bit of advice. Stop trying so hard. Let him go. If you don't—and if something else happens to blast this case wide open, as it might—you'll get hurt even worse."

"I don't care," Lynn said. "Griff hasn't anyone else on his side, no one at all. He needs someone and I belong there—even if it's the wrong side."

He wagged his head at her—*no use trying to talk sense to a woman in love*—and backed out of the drive while she went into the house.

Her father was not at home. While in her bedroom upstairs, changing into pale blue tapered slacks and matching jersey, she heard the front entrance open. Her father came in, talking in his familiar chesty tones, and Dick Carrick's smooth voice answered. Hearing her step on the stairs, they dropped their discussion. As she came into the living-room Carrick greeted her with a self-confident smile and Spencer Armstead with a look of grave expectancy.

"You've seen Griff. Tim told me how you worked it, so he couldn't duck you again as he did yesterday. Very neat, Lynn. Tim also said Griff was behaving peculiarly—suspiciously."

"Dad, I'm trying to be fair. Griff behaved like a proud young man in a humiliating position. It hurt him to confess failure, but he's facing it—that and the tough problem of having to start all over again from scratch. He didn't say anything suspicious—not a single thing to show guilty knowledge. As I told Dan, he can't even guess why he's suspected—he doesn't know anything at all about the kidnapping."

Carrick said sceptically, "That's highly unlikely, isn't it, Lynn? In fact, it's hardly possible for so much evidence of a crime to point to a man who's totally ignorant of it."

"Failure?" Spencer Armstead asked before Lynn could answer Carrick. "How do you mean that?"

"Griff's given up all hope of developing Pelican Key."

"Naturally," Lynn's father said. "What else can he do? He can't possibly account for the ransom money legitimately. He won't dare use it now. It would be tantamount to a confession."

"I suspect," Carrick put in, "that Poole may have had an underworld connection with a fence who would have exchanged the hot money for cold—at a heavy discount, of course. When Poole died, that pipe-line may or may not have been cut off. It hardly matters. As Spence says, developments have robbed the ransom money of all value as far as Griff's purpose is concerned. It might as well be a hundred thousand in Confederate bills."

"He's left with no choice at all," Spencer Armstead insisted, "—forced to let Pelican Key go."

"But Griff made his decision days ago, Dad. That was what he came here to tell me Wednesday night, before there was any reason to suspect him."

"He said that today," her father pointed out, "but he didn't mention it to me then. Can't you see, Lynn, it's an afterthought, a cover-up?—glib enough but hardly convincing."

Lynn lifted her chin. "Seeing Griff and listening to him has changed my way of thinking about him. Some of the evidence just doesn't hold water any more. For instance, that empty deodorizer can on the trash heap. If it means anything at all, it helps to show that Griff *isn't* guilty."

Carrick asked, half smiling, "How can you possibly figure that?"

"You've said all along that the two men who kidnapped me were very smart operators. They thought of everything in advance, they were careful to cut off every lead. But if you assume that Griff left the can there in plain sight, in a place where we would surely look, it can't be anything but a glaring piece of carelessness—which is too inconsistent to believe. I think the can was planted there. Did you find fingerprints on it—Griff's?"

"Only smudges. Clear-cut prints don't turn up as often as people generally think." Carrick stopped smiling. "Nobody could have planted it there, Lynn. There are several different brands of air fresheners on the market. But nobody, not even you, knew what brand had been used."

"Alec Poole did," Lynn answered at once. "We saw Poole and his girl in his boat coming from the general direction of Pelican Key. If it was planted, he certainly was the one who did it. But for what reason? He wouldn't have dared to try to frame his own accomplice. It would backfire—the accomplice could squawk and incriminate Poole. What the can really shows is that Griff *wasn't* the accomplice."

"It could have been planned as a double-cross," Carrick said. "Isn't it just as logical to assume the reverse, that in attempting to save his own skin Griff would refuse to talk? Poole would count on that, and meanwhile make off with the entire ransom instead of half."

Lynn stood her ground. "But there are other things that don't fit. The way the money was handled—— The kidnappers collected the ransom at about four o'clock in the morning. They brought it to the hide-out, counted it, divided it into two equal packages. It was almost dawn then. They hadn't enough time left to go to Pelican Key and back—they would have had to make the return trip in daylight and they couldn't risk being seen together. They had to get back under cover and wait. But Griff needn't have waited at all. He's the one person, the *only* person in town who could have taken the money across the bay at any time of the day or night without the slightest risk or question. He could have done it twenty-four hours before the search even started. But the real kidnappers couldn't, and that's exactly why they made Griff their tool. Don't you see? All this shows he *wasn't* a party to it."

"Who says Griff was merely a tool? Griff himself?" Spencer Armstead was frowning at his daughter. "Naturally! He's an unconscionable liar. The tape recording—his answers to Dan Teague's questions—is proof of that."

Was there nothing she could say in Griff's defence that they couldn't twist to point against him?

"There's something else," she persisted. "You told me how you'd put Dan Teague and Bob Sage on the alert, how they were all set to go into action the minute you gave them the signal. You were very careful to keep your

171

plans perfectly quiet. But the kidnappers had wind of it in advance; they were prepared. That's why they used Griff's boat and that's how Poole was able to trick Dan with his fake alibi. Poole couldn't have learned this for himself, so he must have heard it from his accomplice. But how could Griff have known that?"

"Very simple," Carrick said. "Griff is pals with the Coast Guardsmen and the police force both. A leak, that's all. Or if not that, then his visit to Teague's office told him —he simply put two and two together. In fact, I can't think of anyone who was in a better position to read the signs." Carrick was showing a rare trace of impatience. "You've got it backwards, Lynn. The fact that the kidnappers were forewarned is not a point in Griff's favour— actually it's a score against him."

Lynn was contending with intangibles which were as immovable as mountains. Her father's inflexible prejudice against Griff. Carrick's firm conviction that so much evidence could not point to an innocent man. Dan Teague's wounded self-esteem. Blind emotional attitudes—and lacking even "one good solid fact," Lynn was powerless to change them.

Even the well-meaning Mr. Clane—— She was certain Clane actually had seen Poole's accomplice running for cover with a bundle of ransom money, yet he had obligingly accepted as gospel an alternative suggested by the chief of police whose favour he valued. And Vina Daly—— Because Poole and his accomplice had carefully avoided meeting in her presence, because she had seen Poole speaking to Griff about something she could not overhear, Vina had jumped to an appallingly wrong conclusion. Human errors—but lacking "one good solid fact," Lynn was helpless to correct them.

Worst of all were doubts of her own which she could not explain away—principally Griff's presence at the hide-out at the very time when the ransom money was being divided. And her wedding-ring, still lying concealed there as an unquestionable mark of identification. She dreaded to mention it, still more to succeed in finding it.

Carrick was speaking again. "You're overlooking something which simply is not debatable, Lynn. That telephone call I saw Griff making at one-thirteen in the morning—the call recorded here at the same minute. How do you account for that? It couldn't——"

"Couldn't possibly be a coincidence!" Lynn cried it out. "I know!" Yet—— Either Griff was the glib and unconscionable liar her father believed him to be, or else something was very wrong about that business of the telephone call. There *had* to be something wrong about it—if only she could find out what it was.

"Dick—— You and Tim were with Dad Wednesday night. It was just past midnight when Griff came. Then, after he left—— How did it go?"

Carrick sounded bored as he recounted it again. "Tim and I thought the snatchers might be watching the house and that a message might come sooner if we cleared out. Tim headed for home. He'd walked over, only two blocks, and didn't want a lift back. Griff had headed for Gulf Boulevard, also walking. I'd decided to keep an eye on him, so I followed him in my car. He'd parked his pick-up truck in the lot behind the Beachcomber Bar. I followed him, keeping a block or two back, until he stopped in front of the police office. Then, when he went on, I followed him again until he reached home. As I've already explained, I was able to watch him through a window. After pacing around a few minutes, he took up the phone——"

"Wait. Dad—— Exactly what was the message?"

Distastefully Spencer Armstead quoted it from memory. "'That's better. Keep them out. Stay alone there. Later tonight.'"

"Yes!" Suddenly elated, Lynn had it. "When Griff left, Dick and Tim were still here. He had no way of knowing whether or not they intended to stay. He walked straight to his truck, then drove on. He wasn't aware that by then Dick and Tim had gone. But the man who gave you that message knew it. 'Keep them out—stay alone.' That man *knew* it and Griff didn't—so it couldn't have been Griff who phoned here!"

Spencer Armstead shrugged impatiently. "A good guess, that's all—lucky and logical."

"Don't forget, Lynn, your father, receiving the call, noted the time as one-thirteen." Carrick's voice had turned chilly. "*I saw* Griff making a call at exactly the same minute. We each made note of the time independently. Now. Ruling out coincidence, because the odds against it are far too great, what other possibility is left? Do you believe your father and I are deliberately fabricating this evidence?"

"Of course she doesn't!" Spencer Armstead blurted, his voice forceful with indignation. "Let's have no more of this nonsense, Lynn. Accept the truth. There's still not a single piece of evidence to point suspicion anywhere else. All of it points to Griff and to Griff only. The man is guilty, treacherous, utterly unworthy of your smallest thought. I'll not hear you—you, his victim!—defending him again."

But she was still certain there must be another explanation. Not guilt on Griff's part—not falsification on her father's or Carrick's—not coincidence—but somehow something——

"And I'll remind you of this, Lynn," her father added emphatically. "Griff has in his possession one hundred thousand dollars belonging to me. Perhaps you can persuade him to return it. If so, that will be the easy way out. Otherwise it will be impossible to keep this matter under control—and regardless of the consequences to Griff I damned well intend to get my money back."

The door gong sounded. Spencer Armstead ignored it. Dazed by his ultimatum, Lynn did not move. It was Dick Carrick who opened the entrance. Turning then, Lynn saw in amazement the man standing in the doorway was Bill Rockwood.

Bill! Here? He had never before entered Spencer Armstead's house. Striding in now, he brushed Carrick aside and came straight to Lynn's father.

"You forgot," Rockwood said, contempt in the twist of his mouth. "Ken Simpson is an old friend of mine. I helped him get his bank started when Belle Loma was nothing but an out-of-the-way fishing village. I knew he wouldn't lie to me about this fancy syndicate he's fronting for. I asked him straight out if you were one of the top men in it. He didn't say yes. But he couldn't deny it and that told me what I wanted to know. You and your greedy friends with the money-bags, you and your high-and-mighty wire pulling—*you're* the reason Griff has been balked at every step."

Lynn was staring incredulously at her father. He was wordless, suddenly sickly pale, avoiding her eyes.

"I won't deal with this so-called Belle Loma Associates as long as you're a part of it," Rockwood said flatly. "I'm broke, and if I have to do it to eat I'll cut up my island and sell it lot by lot—but not one square inch of it to you. I'll go farther, and you can thank your under-handed double-dealing for this. I won't sell to any syndicate at all unless Griff has a damned good fair-and-square share in it. How he gets it will be up to the others, but he'll have to have it before I'll even start listening to them. Those are my final terms. Tell that to your boy Hampden."

Bill Rockwood turned his back on Spencer Armstead. The entrance slammed shut behind him. Carrick sat looking down, stoop-shouldered and shamefaced. Lynn's father turned away, a stricken man.

"It's business," he said with a lame gesture. "Business."

She could not answer him. For a moment she went on staring at him as if at a stranger—this man who had denounced her husband as treacherous! . . . She went quietly into the vestibule——

"Lynn! Where are you going?"

"I'm going to Griff."

—and quietly out of the house.

In the dark bedroom the telephone began ringing. As Griff reached towards it Lynn squeezed his arm.

"Don't answer. It's probably Dad. Let it ring, darling."

She lay contentedly at his side, her head nestling on his bare shoulder, smiling when the ringing stopped. . . .

Then, she did not know how much later, there was a knocking on the door, too loud and too demanding to be ignored. She swung out of bed and found Griff's robe. Wrapping it snugly about her body, she went the familiar way into the living-room. With the lighting of lamps the knocking stopped. Before opening the door Lynn looked back at Griff. He was coming towards her, barefoot and bare-chested, in a hastily found pair of dungarees.

Spencer Armstead stood on the doorstep, glowering in, his face puffy with sullen rage. Behind him Chief of Police Teague frowned in the light.

"You can't possibly realize what you've done," Spencer Armstead said.

"I've told Griff everything that's happened, everything about it. He swears you're wrong about him, all of you, I believe him."

"Lynn——" Dan Teague said gently. "The real reason we came—— The case has taken a bad turn. Tim Hampden had word a short while ago from the Palmport Hospi-

tal. About his brother Hal—— Hal never recovered con-
sciousness. He's dead."

The night air drifting in the open door turned icy. Griff
came closer to Lynn's side. She found his hand and held it
tightly.

"I'm terribly sorry."

"There can't be any mistake about it this time," Teague
said. "You were an eye-witness. It's out-and-out murder
now."

"Out-and-out murder," Spencer Armstead said. "You
cannot possibly realize what an outrageous thing you've
done. Coming here—staying here with the man guilty of
killing——" He choked on his fury.

Lynn was gazing at the chief. "What are you going to
do?"

"It's pretty much out of my hands. Paul Shellam
phoned me—the county prosecutor. He's coming over—
on his way now, wanting to hear what the evidence is.
First Alec Poole, now Hal Hampden—— Shellam can
add. And he'll probably reopen the Poole case. He's a
man who wants action."

Dan Teague turned away. Spencer Armstead's eyes
were fixed on Lynn with a dark demand.

"There can be no question what *you're* going to do,
Lynn. You'll come back with me now."

He walked stiffly to the black sedan he had left parked
in the street and stopped beside it, waiting for her. Without a glance at Griff, quickly loosening her hand from his,
Lynn followed her father.

"I came here because I belong here—and I do realize
what I've done. I wouldn't undo it if I could. It was right.
It was legal too—you can't charge Griff with that. Especially because I was an accessory before the fact."

She went back into her home and the arms of the man
they had called a murderer.

CHAPTER XVII

THEY HAD DRESSED and Lynn had made a pot of coffee. Facing each other across the table in the breakfast nook, they felt caged and at the same time lost. This house was without security; it was awash in a flood of suspicion.

Griff quickly emptied his cup and pushed himself to his feet. As he moved restlessly about the kitchen Lynn's troubled gaze followed him.

"Somewhere in this town there's a man, a killer with a bundle of crooked money. The chief of police isn't even trying to find him. Dan, your father, and the others don't even believe he exists. Nobody does except you and me, and we don't know where to look for him. But there must be something to work on, somewhere to start. I can't just wait around here like a sitting duck until the D.A. comes gunning for me."

"If I know Paul Shellam, he won't waste any time," Lynn said. "He's aggressive, ambitious, hard-hitting— and Dad won't be able to muzzle him. He'll crack down on Vina Daly the first thing—corner her, work on her until he pulls her story out of her. When Paul hears what she told me about you——"

"I won't stand a ghost of a chance after that."

"Griff, it *must* apply to somebody other than you. Vina was mistaken, dreadfully mistaken in jumping to the conclusion that you were Poole's partner. But she couldn't be mistaken about what Poole let slip by him. It's someone anxious to raise big money to put into Pelican Key as soon as your option expires, because once it's developed it will be a gold mine—someone anxious to buy into the syndicate."

178

"Somebody without much money who needs a lot of it in a hurry—like me." Griff smiled wryly. "Who else?"

"It could be almost anybody in Dad's circle except Dad himself. But we can narrow it down. Remember, Poole was forewarned. He and his partner knew a search would start the minute I was safely back home. Dick had planned it out with Dad's approval and Tim's help." Colour left Lynn's cheeks. She had brought herself to a possibility that repelled her. "The leak could have come from inside my father's home."

"But not from him, certainly. Tim Hampden or Dick Carrick? They both have enough dough to get in on the syndicate deal without having to pull off a kidnapping."

"No. Tim's business hasn't done at all well, and it shows. His office is a hole in the wall, he drives clients around in a three-year-old car that needs a paint job, and he has no secretary—just a teen-ager, part time, to answer the phone when he's out. He refuses to join in with the Board of Realtors' multiple listing service—he insists on handling nothing but exclusives, and he's suffering for it because there are too few of them, yet he sticks to it as a matter of principle. Another thing, he wants to specialize in developments. The syndicate deal is his first good break along that line. He probably shaved his agent's commission in order to land it. He needs that commission pretty badly, but even if he didn't, and if he put it into the syndicate instead, his share would amount to comparatively little."

Lynn was sickened by her own thinking. Many circumstances pointed to Tim Hampden. She remembered a telling point her father had made: "There's a certain element of vengefulness and vindictiveness in this crime." Spencer Armstead had not disapproved of her engagement to Tim; married to her, with her resources, Tim could have prospered—but Griff had cut him out. Lynn could not doubt

179

that she had left a deep hurt in Tim and that later, after leaving Griff, she had aggravated it because she had turned, not back to Tim, but to Hal.

Lynn shivered, recalling the first moment of terror when the two snatchers had closed in on her. Had it been Tim who had held her, himself helpless to intervene, while watching Poole savagely attacking Hal? Tim had been unable to conceal his heartsickness—and was its real source his need to play the game through with the brute who had left Hal all but dead in the gutter? Then, still later, immediately following the explosion, had the fatal blows to Poole's head been driven not so much by greed as by a fury of retaliation? . . . Lynn closed her eyes, shivering again. It fitted too well.

Griff was speaking. "You don't mean Dick Carrick too? He's a shining success as a lawyer—pulls in whopping big fees."

"Yes. But he lives up to every cent of his income and more. That impressive office of his in Palmport, and his big staff there, add up to a terrific overhead. His smaller office here in Belle Loma is all show—it has always operated in the red, yet Dick likes to seem prosperous enough for both. His huge house, his big car, his boat—he's a big spender, and even at that Julie tops him with her closets full of expensive clothes and her lavish entertaining. Dick's buried under his unpaid bills. Of the two, Tim's probably better off. Griff——"

Lynn had left the table. She had caught Griff's agitation. This, she felt, was a detestable choice—and to judge Griff's innocence in terms of a friend's guilt—but it must be faced.

"Something about Dick bothers me. He's sympathetic with Dad, of course—having Dad as an old friend and an important client, too, could account for that. But he seems *too* convinced. He makes so much of that telephone call, especially by insisting it could never in this world be a coincidence."

"The hell of it is, I can't help agreeing with that," Griff said. "There's no record of the call I made, so he's got me there—unless we can figure it out in some other way."

"There has to be another way. If it wasn't coincidence, then—— Was it planned in advance? No, that's out of the question too. Nobody could have possibly foreseen that you would pick up your phone at that minute on impulse. So what else can it be?" Lynn's eyes went round. "A sudden inspiration! Griff! It was done by someone who saw you using your phone, and thought quickly, and had the chance then and there——"

She swung about to a window. It looked out on Belle Loma Way, the bay front, the lights of the marinas weaving twinkling patterns on the water. She blurted, "Yes!" and suddenly she was snatching the door open.

Griff ran after her, out through the gate and along the sea-walled sidewalk. One block north of their home, the municipal pier, busy by day with sight-seers, fishermen, and charter boats, was closed down for the night. Lynn stopped short at the cement steps leading up to the weathered planking. There, at the near end of a row of wooden lockers containing outboard motors, stood a glass-walled telephone booth.

They looked back, through the lighted windows of their living-room.

Lynn pressed her head to Griff's shoulder, trying not to cry. "It's so ridiculous—so simple now and so awful. You see, Griff? The message Dad received had to come from someone who knew he was alone. There are only three possibilities—Dick and Tim both knew, or it might have been someone else who'd seen them leaving the house. But Dick—by his own word, Dick was here."

"Sure!" Griff said. "He saw me pick up the phone.

That gave him the bright idea. He made the call to your father from this booth and noted the time *he* put it through."

"It's so easy to see now—and I so hate seeing it, except that it helps you."

"We'll face him with it," Griff said. "We'll go to his place right now and have it out."

A voice, startling in its unexpectedness, spoke from the sidewalk behind them.

"That won't be necessary."

Dick Carrick was standing there beside his car, as unruffled and self-confident as always, sardonically smiling.

Lynn came closer to Griff's side, feeling a tremble of uncertain fear as Carrick approached them.

"I heard that. It's an ingenious explanation, Lynn. The trouble is, it's all wrong. When I saw Griff making his call I was watching from the sidewalk near the house. Afterwards I didn't come anywhere near this phone booth."

Griff's mouth thinned wryly. "That's easy to say. Dan Teague has to have corroboration of what I tell, so how about you? Got any way of proving you didn't get tricky with this phone?"

"No." Carrick's answer came easily. "But then I don't need it. I don't happen to be a suspect."

"As far as I'm concerned, this makes you a damn good suspect," Griff said. "If I didn't make that call, and if you didn't, who else did? Who else *could* have made it?"

"Pure sophism, that question." Carrick's shrug dismissed it. "Lynn, I've done my best to help you and your father. I came here just now to talk to you. I was sitting there in my car wondering how to make you understand what an extremely foolish thing——"

Griff broke in. "Then why not come to the house? Why stop a block away? You were watching the place again. What for? A chance to plant that tape recorder of yours so you can hear how much we're finding out?"

Carrick went on smoothly, ignoring Griff and shaking his head at Lynn. "The position you're putting yourself into shocks me. Legally it will turn this case into a shambles. The newspapers will have a field day making the worst sort of sensationalism out of it. Think of that, at least for Spencer's sake, before it's too late."

Lynn said quietly, "It's too late now."

"Surely you realize Hal's death—murder, Lynn!—takes the case out of our control entirely. You can't help Griff, not against such overwhelming evidence, but you will bring disaster down on yourself. Too late? No. I'm going to take you back to Spence."

"Let her alone," Griff said. "With Lynn, I've got a chance of clearing myself. That's what you're really thinking of. You don't want that."

Carrick ignored him again. "Come back, Lynn."

She shook her head. "I can't go back."

"At least you should talk it over with your father and me." Carrick put his hand on her arm. "You can't deny us that little. Just for an hour or two, then, if you insist——"

Without volition Griff's fists had closed hard. He saw this was another trick, as transparent as it was underhanded. Within an hour or two, perhaps sooner, he would probably be under arrest, jailed, cut off from the help which only Lynn could give him.

"Let her alone!" he said again, moving closer to Carrick.

A metallic banging noise from across the street stopped him. The door of a car had been slammed shut. They could not find it at once—it was one of several parked in the shadows under a row of pines. Then a woman appeared, a tall, slender woman of patrician bearing, walking slowly and stiffly towards them. When she paused, the light of the street lamp was bright on her sleek black hair and white face.

"Julie," Carrick said, staring at his wife. "You followed me."

"I despise myself for stooping to it." Julia Carrick spoke tersely in a cold fury. "But this has gone on too long now. You've left me all alone at home at night once too often."

"Julie——" Carrick was acutely embarrassed. "Please, not here."

"I didn't really follow you. I held myself back for fully half an hour after you'd left. I knew in advance where I'd find you. Wherever Lynn was, of course."

Carrick abandoned Lynn in an attempt to placate his wife. "Julie, that's enough!"

It was his turn to be ignored. Julia turned her fever-bright eyes on Lynn. "It's not news to you, is it, that he's asked me for a divorce?"

Lynn heard it with dismay. "I didn't know!"

"You never saw a man so upset when Spence phoned to tell him you'd gone back to Griff—like a jealous, moon-struck high-school kid."

"Julie, you're so mistaken! Dick and I? No, there's nothing——"

"I'm not an utter damned idiot, you know," Julia cut in. "I'm well aware of what's been going on. Dick hasn't fooled me with his sneaky comings and goings in the middle of the night."

"*Julie!*"

She whipped her startled husband with a glance that warned him nothing could stop her. "First the whole evening at your house, one evening after another. When
184

he came home and to bed he'd wait until he thought I was sound asleep. Then he'd get up and prowl out of the house, trying so hard not to waken me. He's done it every single night since the beginning of the week—sneaked out early in the morning, then back again hours later—as if I didn't dream what he was doing and where he was going!"

A speechless moment followed—Lynn and Griff staring dumbfounded at Carrick, Carrick too appalled for words, Julia too rageful.

"I'll give you your divorce, Dick Carrick. I'll give it to you right between the eyes."

Always before, Julia had turned contrite after one of these outbursts of temper; but not this time. Carrick watched helplessly as she turned about and stalked back to her car. The door slammed again as violently as before; the head lamps glared. She swung the car into the cross street opposite the pier, and dust flew in the angry red shine of the tail lights.

Carrick searched Lynn's face and Griff's, attempting a rueful smile. "I'm sorry you had to witness that. She knows nothing about the kidnapping, of course. I'm sure I can convince her she's placed the wrong construction on it. But otherwise—about my early-morning comings and goings—she's quite right."

In another amazed silence they let him go on.

"I shouldn't have done it, of course. It was flatly against Spence's wishes—he was being extremely careful, you know—and a dangerous thing, I admit. If the kidnappers had tumbled to it they might have—— But they didn't. I was as careful as possible, and so concerned for you, Lynn, that I had to try to get a lead on them. Unfortunately nothing at all came of it."

"Nothing came of *what*?" Griff asked bluntly.

"I stood watch at various points along the waterfront,

hoping I'd spot the snatchers on the move—something that might tell me where they were hiding Lynn. But as I say, it simply didn't pay off."

"Once before, last Wednesday night, you gave me a song and a dance," Griff said. "I thought then you were pretty fast on your feet. Now I'm damn sure of it."

"You don't believe me? Well, that's the fact of the matter. Disprove it if you can." Carrick opened his car door, turned an appealing look at Lynn, and when she shook her head again he took it as her final refusal. "As for that business of the telephone call—— I still say I didn't make it, but Griff did." His smile was sardonic again. "Sorry, so very sorry, but until you can prove otherwise the record will have it my way."

He left them with that. They could do nothing but stand looking at each other, Lynn tearful, Griff incensed, their first upsurge of hope already killed.

CHAPTER XVIII

THEY WALKED SLOWLY and wordlessly along the sidewalk until they reached their gate. Lynn hesitated there, her hand on Griff's, a question poised in her mind.

"Darling—— There's one more thing to try. I want you to tell me, to remember——" For all her faith in Griff, she could not ask it without a twinge of dread. Somehow his answer must destroy the worst of the uncertainties she had held within herself. But could it? "—remember last Wednesday morning, very early. You were up and around before dawn—weren't you, Griff?"

"Couldn't sleep. No good just lying there tossing in bed, so I left the house. It was still dark."

"Why did you go out?"

"Something to do. You know how some of my gear and material get scattered around at different places where I've done work. I'd be needing some new pilings in a few days, so I went up the bay to the job where I'd left them."

"But *where*, Griff?"

"That promontory north of your father's house—the Peterson place."

The Peterson place? But that was where the men had left her—there on the Peterson pier! To Lynn, Griff's answer was unexpected and inexplicable.

"Will you go back there with me now and show me just what you did?"

"Sure, but why?"

She hoped he didn't know how terribly important it was. "Griff, let's just *go!*"

She turned to her convertible and took the passenger's seat, leaving the wheel to Griff. He gave her a curious look and a small smile. Driving northwards past the municipal pier, then the town offices, he was conscious of her wondering glances.

"I used my car just like this," he said, "and left it on Belle Loma Way where the side road into the site is blocked. Want me to do it that same way again?"

"Please. Exactly the same."

They went on, both puzzled and silent, until Griff swung the car off the pavement alongside a movable barricade of boards bearing a *Keep Out* sign. Lynn jumped out at once. Griff found a flashlight in the glove compartment, then led her into the side road. The narrow point of land projecting into the bay was deserted and entirely dark. On both sides, beyond vacant building lots, the water lapped against the sea wall. They passed skeletal houses on which construction had been abandoned when legal difficulties beset the development. The Peterson house, the farthest, occupying the choicest location, was a low black hulk on the extreme tip of the finger.

Lynn hurried Griff towards it. This house, she recalled, the first to be built, had been nearly completed when the owner, Hugh Peterson, a retired stockbroker, suddenly died. All work was stopped then pending settlement of the estate, and Mrs. Peterson had gone north to live with a sister. In its not-quite-finished condition the house still stood empty and unsold.

Lynn stopped at the foot of a cement walk that angled past the building to the pier behind it. That pier, where the kidnappers had left Lynn lying bound, was one Griff had built. He pointed to a dozen or more pilings, leftovers from the job, lying near the sea wall, and a wooden tool-box, half as large as a coffin and covered with tarpaulin, sitting beside them.

"I just went over there to check the——"

"Do it again, Griff, just as you did it then."

He walked slowly across the bare lot, Lynn following closely, and crushed shell crunched under their shoes with the chilling sound she could not mistake.

"I just looked over the stuff for a few minutes," Griff said, "then went back. That's all."

She knew he didn't understand why she suddenly and joyously hugged him.

"I'm going into that house, Griff."

"It's kept locked."

"Have you a key? Have you ever had one?"

"No."

"Then break in. Anything! Just get me inside it!"

A short branch of the walk ran between the pier and the rear of the building. Lynn found a door. The knob would not turn. Griff bumped a shoulder against the door twice, then shook his head and turned back to the tool-box. He opened the padlock hasped to its lid and came back carrying an axe.

"Don't force this one," Lynn said. "Find another. I'll wait here."

Without question he turned to the front of the house. As she listened to the noises he made her breathing quickened with a sense of impending discovery. Something snapped sharply and Griff called, "Okay, coming through." After another long-seeming minute she heard another sound at the door she faced. Suddenly it was open and Griff was standing just inside with his flashlight shining.

Lynn went in quickly. The air was pungent with the odour of cedar. The unused lumber lay stacked against one cement-block wall.

"A lot of it," Griff said. "Enough for lining all the clothes closets. The builders didn't get around to finishing them. None of the inside doors have been hung either. The smell's all through the house."

There was no way of confining the odour to any other part of the house, and to have removed the boards entirely would have been conspicuous and suspicious.

Quickly taking the flashlight from Griff, Lynn turned its beam about. At one end of the room were two broad metal doors. This was the garage. One other doorway, by which Griff had entered, opened on a small empty room, and Lynn could see another room beyond. Two narrow windows, head high, had been blacked out with pieces of tar paper tacked across the frames. The cement floor was covered with a thin scattering of sand tracked in by the construction men. There, on that side, near the opposite wall, Lynn could imagine herself lying bound.

Again she was reliving the moment of sudden alarm. She knew now that it was Griff's noises in the yard that had brought Alec Poole springing to her side to keep his hands, hard and threatening, on her throat. And the other man? Lynn recalled that in her terror she had been uncertain of his actions. He could not have slipped outside; that move would have exposed him to Griff. The strongest probability she realized now, was that Poole's partner had silently opened the door a crack and had stood there in the dark, warily watching Griff moving about in the open. For a few minutes Griff had been so near!—unaware that he was within reach of Lynn, even unaware that she had been kidnapped. Then he had simply walked away.

"Griff, where did you go from here that morning?"

"Back home."

Then this was the only possibility; this *was* the hide-out.

Lynn stooped, holding the light low, and with her fingers rapidly brushed away the accumulation of sand at the base of the wall. Griff heard her make a sobbing little sound and saw the gleam of gold. She had found her wedding-ring.

Griff reached for it. She caught his arm.

"No. Leave it there."

"Leave it! Why?"

She used her fingers again and the ring was quickly concealed. Straightening, she felt a sense of suffocation. The sharp scent of cedar recalled too strongly the sickening reek of the deodorant. The interminable hours she had helplessly endured here were an experience of pain and fear too vividly remembered. She tugged Griff out through the door, closed it, made certain the latch had sprung into its socket.

"I don't know why," she answered him then. "Not exactly. But it's something we can use somehow—the only thing left."

Back at the car, Griff again took the wheel. Lynn had hurried; she drew herself close to his side, breathless, deeply relieved yet frightened. In finding for herself final assurance of Griff's innocence, she had also brought closer to herself the guilt of the man who had made Poole his accomplice. *"One of them is known to you. His gentleness— knowing you, even liking you——"* Yet there was still no material thing to point to him. Except, possibly, for some small detail they had overlooked, there was still nothing at all.

"Picking that place was smart," Griff said. "For one thing, they didn't have far to take you, and it's so close to your father's house nobody would think of it. For another, they could come and go by either land or water. There are other advantages too, maybe including a certain special reason we don't know about. With Mrs. Peterson living up north now, who's handling the estate here?"

"Dick."

Mention of Carrick reminded Lynn that they were still unable to explain the telephone call at 1.13 except as a fabrication of Carrick's—and that was hopeless proof.

"They were as clever as fiends," Lynn said. "That last night was when they began pointing suspicion at you. Before that they'd probably had no thought of it, but the way you'd behaved gave them something to build on. They began with me, by planting false ideas in my mind. When they carried me out of the garage, instead of going straight from the door to the pier, they wove back and forth to make it seem I was being taken along a winding path like the one on Pelican Key. They put out in the boat and circled back to the same pier to fool me into thinking I'd been brought across the bay. And that can of deodorizer Poole planted on the trash pile—I'm sure he was acting on orders, and in a hurry, because I had made an important point of it." Lynn covered her face with her hands. "It keeps coming back so close to home!"

"But they were getting away clean," Griff said, "so why did they go to the extra trouble of framing me?"

"Until that same night there wasn't any sign of a possible reconciliation between us. Making you a suspect in my eyes would prevent it."

Griff turned a startled look on Lynn. One man was adamantly determined to block a reconciliation—Spencer Armstead. . . . The same thought had not occurred to Lynn. She was smiling at him.

"That idea didn't work, did it, Griff?"

He put his arm around her shoulders, unable to voice his thought that her sweetness could turn into even deeper pain for both of them.

"It's so strange," Lynn said. "With all their cleverness they were unlucky. First Hal, the way he surprised them, then his dying—the fuel leak in your boat and the explosion—and the missing half of the ransom money may be worthless to the man who has it. Actually the whole carefully laid plan is a failure."

"Except that Poole's pal is still getting away with it by miles," Griff said. "Getting away with a kidnapping and two murders. And I'm straight in line for the rap."

Suddenly Lynn sat up. She spoke urgently.

"Griff! Turn here. Now!"

He responded without thinking. The car was already swinging into the dark cross street before he realized where they were. He had driven past the business section of Belle Loma, preoccupied, scarcely noticing; now they were only two blocks north of their home. He let the car crawl, staring wonderingly at Lynn.

"The police car is there in front of the house," she explained quickly. "Dan Teague and another man are standing beside it, waiting. I think the other man is Paul Shellam."

The county prosecutor. Griff stopped the car.

"They're ready to grab me. But I'm damned well not ready to *be* grabbed."

"Go back to the Peterson place," Lynn said. "If you can make it on foot——"

He slid out quickly. "I'll make it."

"I'll go on and try my best to make them see. I think there's something I can do that may show them——" He was kissing her. "Wait there, Griff. I'll come soon."

He hurried away through the shadows under the pines. Until he turned from sight at the far corner she watched him, feeling a sinking sense of defeat. What were they to gain by this move? Wouldn't it merely delay the inevitable, Griff's arrest—and not for long?

She had located and identified the hide-out, but that fact would be of no help to Griff. They would ask her *how* she had found it. She could not explain without admitting that Griff had led her to it. He had been able to do this through circumstances incriminating to him, which she had concealed. If she revealed them now, they would be no less incriminating—her original interpretation of them could be taken as valid, further proof of his guilt; and Griff's own story must again go unsupported except by her explanation, which would be considered biased. In the minds of those closest to Lynn, Griff was still the sole suspect; the prejudices against him remained as strong, the evidence as black. And time was running out.

CHAPTER XIX

ALONE IN THE police car, Dan Teague led the way into the driveway of the Armstead home. Lynn followed in her convertible, uneasily aware of the indignation of the man sitting beside her. Paul Shellam had intensely earnest eyes and a manner of hair-trigger decisiveness. Within one minute by the clock, having met Shellam and Teague in front of her home, Lynn had offended the prosecutor by refusing point-blank to tell him where Griff might be found.

They stopped behind two other cars in the driveway—Carrick's costly hard-top and Tim Hampden's old coupé. Going in, they found Carrick and Hampden with Spencer Armstead in the living-room. Lynn immediately became the focal point of the troubled eyes of the five men. For a moment none of them spoke, and their silence was censure.

"I'd better warn you all," Lynn said quietly. "You're going to have trouble with me. I've stopped listening to your arguments against Griff. I'm on my husband's side for keeps."

"This is unheard of!" Paul Shellam blurted. "Mr. Armstead, your daughter is making this case a legal nightmare. We have one suspect, and conclusive evidence of his guilt, yet this girl will not believe he isn't innocent. The victim of the crime insists on making herself the key witness for the defence!"

"Lynn," her father said heavily, "you simply haven't stopped to think. Such utter disloyalty to me—such complete disregard of your friends and your own welfare—— I never would have thought you capable of it."

"I can't help it, Dad. It has to be one way or the other. I admit, what I'm doing would be unforgivable if Griff were really guilty. But I know he isn't."

"You see?" Shellam was bristling. "Well! It won't stop me, Mr. Armstead. I'll press the case to a conviction in spite of her." He added as a stinging afterthought, "To make it even worse, she's practically harbouring him as a fugitive. She admits knowing where he is but she won't tell me. It's sheer romantic folly. If she thinks she can accomplish something by it, I'd like to know what and how."

"Sit down and listen to me," Lynn said, "and you'll hear just that."

For another moment they gazed at her wordlessly. Shellam, shrugging as if to say *Well, it probably won't hurt to humour her*, was the first to sit. Lynn waited until all the five men were in chairs. She studied their faces. Her father's expression was one of soul-sick regret. Tim Hampden's, now that his brother was dead, revealed a deeper bitterness and darker brooding. Teague's was stony and Shellam's resentfully sceptical. Among them all Dick Carrick's was the least unpleasant; his self-confidence unshaken, he had resigned himself to Lynn's decision. . . . They were five judges who had already arrived at a verdict. They would listen, but it would take more than words to force a reversal.

"You've kept saying there's no evidence against anyone but Griff, but I'm sure there is. There simply has to be evidence somewhere pointing to the man who made Alec Poole his accomplice. There's only one question really—where is it? I'm going to tell you how to find it."

"Indeed," Shellam said dryly. "We have here a well-trained police chief, a lawyer who was formerly an FBI agent, and a competent prosecuting attorney, and we are about to be instructed by——"

"By the victim who knows more about the inside of the case than any of you. Dick——"

Carrick lifted his head with a jerk. "Yes, Lynn."

"You'll remember I told you, when we went over to the old shack on Pelican Key, I had a way of making sure whether or not it was the hide-out. It wasn't. I didn't explain then how I knew, but we've come to the point now where I'll have to tell you. I want that hide-out to be found. And when it is found, there won't be any question about it—I'll know it for sure."

"But, Lynn," Carrick said, "you were blinded the whole

while and you never saw it. On the basis of your description it might be any one of a hundred different places."

"And just how do you suggest we go about finding it?" Shellam put in, "—fine-comb the whole bay area? We'd need a small army for the job. It would take days—weeks."

"That's the only way, yes—search the whole bay front, every mile of it. You do have the men for it—the Palmport police, plus the police of all the towns up and down the Gulf beaches, and the FBI, too, if you want their help. It's somewhere—it can and must be found because it's a very important part of the case—so important that my husband's life may depend on it. I'm not being melodramatic when I say that—it's true."

Shellam squirmed in his chair. "Suppose, for the sake of argument, we do it and come up with half a dozen or more possibilities? Just how will you know which is the right one?"

"This is how."

Lynn held up her left hand. As she explained how she had used her wedding-ring, without the kidnappers' knowledge, to mark the hide-out, subtle tensions came into the faces of the five. The changes were unreadable to Lynn—except that the lift of Paul Shellam's eyebrows seemed to indicate admiration for her ingenuity.

"All right," the prosecutor said. "Assume we've found it—your ring has clinched that point. It's a fishing shack or an unoccupied house—a place anyone might have used for the purpose, including your husband. What has it proved except that the kidnappers kept you prisoner there?"

"Evidence!—that's what I'm getting at," Lynn said. "They used it from Sunday night until Thursday morning—three days and four nights. During that period they came and went, singly and together, many times. They must have left signs of themselves. They couldn't possibly have avoided it. Fingerprints, footprints, something else left behind—but there simply has to be *something*."

Shellam's eyebrows went up a shade higher.

"Dick——" Lynn turned back to him. "You know much more about this than I do. The FBI crime lab in Palmport would help, wouldn't it? Don't they have the means of finding traces and testing them—unavoidable traces so slight that a crook wouldn't even think of them, no matter how smart he might be?"

"That's quite true," Carrick said. "The FBI labs have pulled off some amazing successes. For example, a man may be identified by an analysis of the dried saliva on a cigarette butt. Hair is distinctive, and fibres, microscopic debris from clothing. Also tiny particles of leather or rubber left by shoes on a rough floor. As you say, even the most intelligent criminal isn't educated to all these scientific techniques, and even if he were it would do him no good. He can be convicted on evidence invisible to the naked eye." He turned to the prosecutor. "No doubt of it, Paul, she has a strong point there."

Shellam abruptly changed his tune; finding himself backed into a corner, he had to justify himself. "I keep up to the minute with most advanced methods of crime investigation, you know. Frankly, Lynn, I didn't need your suggestion. I had intended to organize such a search. Starting it tonight is hardly feasible, but I've already taken a few steps towards getting it under way tomorrow morning."

Lynn saw Dan Teague's small puckered smile. . . . Immediately it faded. This was going to mean a big job of work for the chief and his men, and in spite of his sympathy for Lynn he had no faith in it.

"Tell me this, Lynn." Shellam had come decisively to his feet, his intense eyes on her. "Considering the other evidence, this will very likely produce still more of it against your husband. What will be your position then?"

Lynn said simply, "It won't."

Scanning the uncertain faces of the five men, she kept to herself her real hope, that they would never need to begin the search—that they would have the true answer before morning.

Lynn had finished.

"Am I under arrest?" she asked Shellam. "Or may I go home now?"

"Keep yourself available, that's all," and a wave of his hand dismissed her.

Four of the men rose and drew together. As they began discussing the plan, Dan Teague stood apart, shaking his head at Lynn. She tugged at his sleeve and said softly, "Come with me." He shrugged and followed her out through the entrance.

"It's hopeless," he said as he closed the door behind them. "If it isn't a waste of time, it'll nail the case on Griff. You just don't realize what you're doing."

"But I do know, Dan, and I need your help. Please follow me in your car."

She hurried on to her convertible before he could answer. When she had the car started, rolling it along the circular driveway, she saw that Teague, like Shellam, had decided it would do no harm to humour her. The headlights of the police car shone behind her as she crossed the Drive and drove on to Belle Loma Way.

When she reached the barricaded side road she turned left into a cross street, stopped and slipped out. Teague, his car directly behind hers, stayed at the wheel, puzzled.

"I don't want anyone to know where we've gone."

They left both cars dark in that inconspicuous spot. Lynn's hand on Teague's arm hurried him across the highway and past the barricade. As they approached the Peterson house she sensed a rising guardedness in him. She guided him along the walk to the door in the rear wall of the garage. It was locked. She tapped her knuckles on it.

"Griff? Let me in."

An empty moment passed. She was about to knock again when the spring bolt clicked free. The door opened, revealing Griff with a burning flashlight in his hand. At sight of Teague he stiffened and turned his bewildered eyes on Lynn. She pushed Teague inside, closed the door, and made sure it was locked again.

The light of the flash reflecting from the floor threw distorting shadows on their faces. Teague stood frowning at Griff with his hand on his holstered gun.

"What's this mean?" he asked of Lynn. "You knew he was here, so why did you bring me? It's my job to take him in."

"Not yet. A little time won't matter now. We're going to wait here. This is where they kept me, Dan."

Teague took the light from Griff and swung it curiously across the walls and over the stack of cedar boards. He watched as Lynn uncovered her wedding-ring and stooped in astonishment for a closer look. She concealed it again, straightened, and searched the chief's face.

"There may or may not be evidence here, Dan—I don't know. The important thing is that the guilty man is afraid the FBI lab men might find some. But the lab men can't even start work until after I've identified a certain place as the hide-out. They won't bother to examine places I can't identify—there would be no point in it. Everything depends on where my ring is found. And if it isn't found anywhere, then the whole operation is stymied and Poole's partner will still be safe."

"Ah?" Teague said. "How do I know this isn't some

stunt you and Griff have cooked up—some kind of fancy smoke-screen?"

"You don't," Lynn said. "You'll have to see for yourself. That's why you're here. Now we're going into the next room, and we'll keep the flashlight off and wait."

Rain was falling. It had begun almost an hour ago—not one of the brief tropical downpours that characterize Florida summers, but a thin splattering fall, typical of autumn, that promised to continue throughout the night.

Now and then Teague had flicked the flashlight at his wrist-watch. Now he did it again. "Two hours," he grumbled.

Their eyes had become adjusted to the almost total lack of light. A faint glow from the neon signs on the highway came through two wet windows. Lynn, sitting on the floor, could see the dim form of Teague leaning wearily against the opposite wall and Griff restlessly walking in a circle. The waiting was empty and wearing and, to the two men, interminable. Only two hours! Lynn had waited here, bound into a bone-aching torment, for more than seventy. She had learned to wait.

Teague complained. "This won't work. How can it? The case shapes up in either one of two ways. Either Griff and Poole pulled it. Or it was Griff and Bill Rockwood."

Griff halted. "Bill? What're you talking about?"

"I've been thinking it over. Been hearing things too. Talk gets around in a small town like this one. I know about the syndicate that wants to buy Pelican Key. I've heard your father's in on it, Lynn. And I know how Bill Rockwood hates him. Well, Griff and Bill got together on a plan to abduct you and collect a hell of a fat ransom. Then they'd be all set. Your father would have lost his money and be out of the deal. Bill and Griff together would have enough to get going on the development. It figures out pretty neatly."

"Any way you figure it, I'm in it," Griff said, an edge on his voice. "I wasn't, but Poole was. Have you forgotten him?"

"No. Poole fits too. He had a way of prowling around at all odd hours of the night. So he happened to see something—you or Bill coming or going from this hide-out, if this was it. He smelled something big cooking and he watched. He saw you hiding the money in your boat and knew you'd soon be smuggling it across the bay. That gave him a bright idea of his own. He waited for you, far enough out so there'd be no witnesses, then waylaid you. Piracy. There was a fight and you stopped him with a fire extinguisher over the head. Then you had a dead body to account for and you thought you could do it by blowing up your own boat. You intended to swim on to Pelican Key with the two bundles, but you'd taken a beating and you couldn't make it."

Lynn was gratified to hear Griff answering with an argument she herself had used in his behalf. "Bill and I wouldn't have needed to hide the money on my boat. We could have got it across to Pelican Key any time we wanted to, and buried it back in the jungle where nobody could find it."

"The money had to be hidden somewhere. Lynn's story would make Pelican Key the most likely place. You were afraid of a search, so you planned to let the search be made, then take the money over afterwards. That explains everything."

"Except the things you're leaving out," Griff said. "Who ran Poole's boat back to the motel pier right after the explosion. What became of the second package of money?"

"I saw Bill Rockwood out on the bay, looking over the floating wreckage. I found one package. He found the other. It's as simple as that."

"You're also leaving out——"

Lynn jumped to her feet. Her suddenness silenced them. She stood motionless and breathless, listening. Through the watery noises of the rain they heard footsteps —slow, even, cautious. Someone was going along the walk towards the rear of the house. At the door in the side of the garage the footsteps stopped.

They heard the little rasping noise of a key sliding into the lock.

With that sound certainty came to Lynn. She knew the identity of the man at the door.

CHAPTER XX

DAN TEAGUE HAD moved soundlessly to a position beside the doorway. Lynn stood back, close beside Griff. The small noises of the rain were a screen; for a moment they could hear nothing through it.

The connecting doorway looked upon blackness. None of the faint light in this room reached into the garage. Lynn held her breath in an effort to listen. A brief loudening of the rain-sounds meant that the outer door had been opened and quickly closed again. Now another footstep, inside this time? Griff and Teague gave no sign; they were tightly still.

Suddenly the man was there. A flickering flame appeared—a cigarette lighter. The man was stooping, a shadowy figure, his back turned. He was holding the lighter low and feeling through the sand at the edge of the floor. They heard him make a grunting sound of satisfaction, saw him pick up the ring.

Teague fired the beam of the flashlight at him.

"Stay right there!"

The man exploded into motion. He whirled, keeping his back to the light as he sprang up, and threw the lighter across one shoulder. The flame cut a streak in the air before it went out. Lynn heard the lighter hit Teague's body.

The man's swiftness took him half-way across the garage before Teague could bawl out another order.

"Hold it! I've got a gun!"

Teague was through the connecting doorway. The outer door banged shut and Teague's momentum crashed him against it. Lynn had started after him. She stopped short, looking around in blank confusion. Where was Griff? She couldn't see him or hear him moving. He was gone.

Teague was snarling at himself, and snatched at the door-knob. Now he yanked the door open and lurched through. Lynn, close behind him, saw the man running along the walk. When he reached the front corner of the house Griff sprang into sight. He had slipped out of the house on the opposite side, using the door he had forced.

The running man attempted to spring aside, to by-pass Griff. Lynn heard two sharp cracking sounds. The man was stopped as if he had struck a wall, his head jerking to one side, then to the other. He began toppling backward, caught himself, then pitched forward and sprawled, his face in the wet crushed shell.

Teague's light stayed on him. Griff stood over him, fists still clenched. Lynn and the chief stopped beside him, half expecting him to spring up again, but he lay still. Griff's blows had registered a clean knock-out.

They stared at a staked sign lying on the ground. In

falling the man had struck it and knocked it flat. It lay with its lettering turned up: *Buy—Hampden Exclusive.*

In the living-room of the Armstead home on Belle Loma Drive, Dick Carrick's tape recorder was operating. Carrick and Teague had brought it from the police office, where Prosecutor Paul Shellam had insisted on questioning Tim Hampden in the absence of the principals. For the first time Lynn, Griff, and her father were hearing Hampden's voice in disheartened confession.

". . . Another reason for the Peterson house. No one else here had a key.

". . . Wednesday night, when Griff came to the Armstead house—— He scared me. I thought he might have got wind of what had happened, and if so he'd be dangerous to us. After he'd left I decided to keep an eye on him, to make sure he wouldn't be getting in our way. I went down to his house, but he wasn't there. I waited on the municipal pier, keeping out of sight, and after a while he drove up in his truck and went in. I was still there when Dick Carrick came along and also began watching him through the living-room windows. I could see Griff moving around in there. When he picked up his phone, the idea struck me. The call he made, which Dick witnessed, and the one I made to the Armstead home, disguising my voice, didn't coincide exactly—they may have been as much as twenty or thirty seconds apart—but a minute is sixty seconds long. . . .

". . . That package contains half the ransom money. It's the one Poole tossed to me from Griff's boat while I was alongside in Poole's. . . . After the explosion, when I saw Poole struggling there in the water—when I heard him pleading with me to help him—— Help him! After what he'd done to Hal? No! That was my chance to pay Poole back for that, and I took it."

Lynn said quickly, "I've heard enough."

Carrick switched the recorder to *Stop*. Griff stood looking at the men who had been so certain of his guilt—Spencer Armstead, Carrick, Teague. What could they say now?

Carrick said nothing. He shook his head as he might shake it after an adverse verdict in the courtroom. *Too bad I lost the case, but it's all in the day's work.*

Spencer Armstead turned to Griff with a look of heartsick compassion; he put his hand on Griff's shoulder in a manner meant to be apologetic, even comradely; he seemed about to speak; but no words came. He turned away again and slowly, wearily, climbed the stairs. What counted the most with Spencer Armstead was not that Griff was cleared, and not that he had recovered one hundred thousand dollars. He had utterly lost Lynn.

Lynn watched uncertainly as Griff turned his gaze on Dan Teague. The chief came to Griff, offering his hand. Griff clasped it and they summoned up a grin for each other. But it was forced, Lynn knew. Perhaps in time their broken friendship would heal; but only time would tell.

"Come on, honey," Griff said. "Let's go home. I mean *home.*" He meant the cottage on Pelican Key.

"Hold on a minute." Teague was extending his hand again, this time palm up. "This was the only good, solid piece of evidence in the whole case, but we won't be needing it."

Griff's grin was broader and warmer as he slipped the wedding-ring on his wife's finger.

"Till death us do part," he said.